The Scribbling Sea Serpent:

A Collection of Strange Tales

Kate Kelly

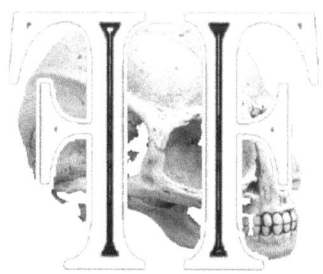

Fortean Fiction

THE SCRIBBLING SEA SERPENT:
A COLLECTION OF STRANGE TALES

Published in Great Britain by CFZ Press 2015

Edited and typeset by Andrew May
Cover by Andrew May and Kate Kelly

Copyright © 2015 by Centre for Fortean Zoology

ISBN: 978-1-909488-28-1

CFZ Press
Myrtle Cottage
Woolsery
Bideford
North Devon
EX39 5QR

www.cfzpublishing.co.uk

STORY CREDITS

Discord © Kate Kelly 2010: First published in *Dark Valentine* # 2, September 2010.

Down to the Sea © Kate Kelly 2011: First published in *Aoife's Kiss*, September 2011.

Grimstone Mire © Kate Kelly 2015: Original to this volume.

Heaven Sent © Kate Kelly 2015: Original to this volume.

High Tide © Kate Kelly 2011: First published in *Jupiter SF* # 31, January 2011.

Icebound © Kate Kelly 2007: First published in *Ruins Terra* (Hadley Rille Books), August 2007.

In the Precinct of Amun-Re © Kate Kelly 2008: First published in *Ruins Metropolis* (Hadley Rille Books), July 2008.

Last Traces © Kate Kelly 2009: First published in *Footprints* (Hadley Rille Books), July 2009.

One in a Million © Kate Kelly 2007: First published in *Hub* # 8, May 2007.

Remember Normandy © Kate Kelly 2015: Original to this volume.

Return to Aller © Kate Kelly 2010: First published as 'Return to Athelnay' in *Sorcerous Signals*, May 2010 and reprinted in *Mystic Signals* # 6, Oct 2010.

Rosemary Lane © Kate Kelly 2007: First published in *The Willows* # 2, July 2007 and reprinted in *Pseudopod*, 22nd February 2009.

Supply Ship © Kate Kelly 2007: First published in *Murky Depths* # 1, September 2007.

Symbionts © Kate Kelly 2010: First published in *The Absent Willow Review*, February 2010.

For James

CONTENTS

THE ORACLE

Aldo Martinelli paused to catch his breath. He gazed back down the stony mountain track along which he had climbed to where the Bay of Naples spread out before him, sunlight shimmering on the sea. The heat was already beginning to beat down on his back and his chest felt tight, his ribcage heaving beneath the damp fabric of his shirt. He pulled off his hat and wiped a handkerchief over his head, thin hair plastered flat against his scalp. He replaced his hat, adjusted the brim to protect his eyes from the glare of the sun on the sea and sighed. It was a beautiful view.

Of course, it had been very different in his youth. The whole area of the bay had been densely populated; Naples, the city of his birth, thronging with people and away from the city a patchwork of vineyards and citrus and olive groves on the rich volcanic soil. He remembered driving through cobbled streets on his Lambretta, cooler than cool, and drinking sweet wine in the Piazzas with his friends.

He had been lucky. He wasn't here when the volcano blew.

From his vantage point on the slopes of Vesuvius Aldo could see the paths that the pyroclastic flows had taken as they cut their swathes of devastation across the vineyards and into the city. Not enough time had passed to heal those scars, neither on the landscape nor in the hearts of the people, and the city that had once been his home was marked only by an expanse of grey ash. How many bodies were buried there people could only begin to guess, for the ash layer was many metres thick. Naples was no more.

Aldo felt tears start to prick behind his eyes as his thoughts lingered – people called Naples the second Pompeii. Pompeii herself was buried and Aldo felt a pang of sadness, grief for the ancient city that had been the subject of so much of his early research; the start of his career in Archaeology now entombed in ash once more.

If he squinted his eyes he could just make out the jumble of whitewashed houses and green trees beyond the plain of ash that marked where Sorrento still stood. Beyond he half imagined that he could see the rugged beauty of the Amalfi coast. That was where he belonged. Not here on this barren slope.

"Dr Martinelli!"

At the sound of his name Aldo turned, lifting his hand to shield his eyes from the sun. One of his research students was scrambling down the side of the volcano towards him, ash and pumice trickling down the slope in tiny rivulets from where his feet landed. Occasionally a larger piece would keep on going.

"Dr Martinelli, I'm so glad you could make it." He stopped in front of Aldo, his teeth a flash of white against skin, tanned dark by the sun. Aldo smiled. Marco was a young man of great promise.

"Quite a climb. I'm not as young as I was. I hope it's going to be worth it."

"Oh, I think it will be."

"Is it the casts?"

Marco shook his head. "No, something else."

He turned and led the way back up the slope, leaving the track that vanished in a slow curve round the flank of the mountain. The surface of the slope was very loose, almost scree, and Aldo felt his feet slipping with every step he took. He leaned heavily on his stick and the sweat began to break out over him once more. There were a hundred questions he wanted to ask, but he didn't have the breath. They would have to wait.

They came on the site quite suddenly. Aldo was surprised, even though he had been here before. It was hidden behind an outcrop of jutting rock where the last great eruption, the one that had buried Naples, had activated a long dormant fault and the shifting strata had exposed the ruin. Until then nobody had known there was a Roman temple here, halfway up the volcano. There were no records of it anywhere, and after the AD 79 eruption, which buried Pompeii had obliterated it, this temple had been forgotten – until the mountain moved once more.

There was very little left of the temple now for the destruction, so high on the volcano's slopes, had been almost complete. No walls stood, and those artifacts they were managing to pull from the pumice were badly distorted, melted by the heat of the pyroclastic flows, crushed by the weight of the ash and tuff that had covered them. Aldo peered round at the outlines of the foundations and the fallen blocks of masonry that remained. Behind was the deep layer of ash where they had poured plaster of Paris into the voids in case they were impressions left by artifacts long decayed, or even by the bodies of the victims of that ancient disaster, like the ones found in Pompeii. Aldo felt a pang of sadness, wondering if someone would make plaster casts of the dead of Naples in two thousand years. He sighed as Marco led him towards the rest of the team.

There were five in all, all archaeology undergraduates from Rome, and they stepped aside as Marco approached.

"It's here," Marco said.

One of the students, the only girl in the group, her long black hair tied back and grey with pumice dust, stepped forwards and handed Aldo a bottle of water. He gulped the tepid liquid and at last felt that he could speak. Marco was pointing to an opening in the ground. It looked very much like a fissure – a natural feature of the barren landscape around them – but for the steps, hewn out of the lava itself, leading down into the blackness.

"Some sort of antechamber?" Aldo suggested.

"Yes." Marco grinned. "But we think it's much older than the Roman temple."

"Really?" He raised his eyebrows and waited for Marco to explain.

One of the other students who had been standing nearby handed a torch to Marco. He switched it on and stepped over to the fissure, the thin beam probing the chasm. Aldo followed and peered down into the gloom.

"Fantastic!" he muttered. The walls that lined the stairs were covered with painted carvings, perfectly preserved, ornate and detailed, paint starting to flake but the colours still vivid. There were figures dancing, praying, couples entwined. And they weren't Roman.

"I see what you mean," he said. "Has anyone been down yet?"

Marco shuffled his feet and didn't answer. Aldo fixed him with a hard stare.

"Who's been down?"

Marco shrugged.

"I'm sorry. We got carried away looking at the murals. Roberto went down."

Aldo glanced round the group, eager to hear what Roberto had seen, but he couldn't see him anywhere. The students shifted uneasily beneath his gaze.

"Where's Roberto?"

Marco ran a hand through his thick black hair. "The devil took him," he said in a whisper.

"What?"

The students nodded their assent. Aldo drew in a slow deep breath. Superstitious fools! Why were people these days so susceptible to believing such nonsense?

"Tell me what happened," he said.

"We were going down," Marco said in hushed tones. "Roberto was ahead of me, and then suddenly there was this strange smell, kind of sweet, and my head began to spin."

Aldo nodded. This was all starting to make sense.

"And then Roberto started screaming and foaming at the mouth and thrashing about with his arms. Then he ran back up the steps and past me. I ran after him, but when I got back up here he was gone." Marco's eyes grew wide and frantic as he spoke. Aldo looked round at the students.

"So where is he now?" he demanded. One of the boys crossed himself. The rest looked decidedly edgy. "Come on. He didn't vanish into thin air did he?" He glared around the group. Fools.

"We don't know," said Marco. "When I got back up here and managed to get my head clear he was nowhere to be seen. The others say he ran off across the rocks."

"And you didn't try to find him or call for help?" Aldo shook his head. What was wrong with people these days? Always looking for a higher cause, never willing to accept that bad things just happen. The destruction of the bay of Naples had hit everyone hard, but there were catastrophes happening all the time. There always had been. These times were not so very different.

"I tell you the devil took him," said Marco. Aldo groaned inwardly. How was he going to explain this one to the authorities? Roberto could be lying out on the volcano slopes, injured, even dead! It didn't bear thinking about!

"I can't believe you can be such idiots! Think about it for Christ's sake! You're archaeology students aren't you? You've all heard of the Oracle at Delphi?"

The students scuffed their feet in the dust and started muttering amongst themselves.

"The Temple of Apollo near Delphi in Greece," said the girl, giving a half smile and shifting her feet in the dust. "The priestess was called the Pythia and she sat in a chamber beneath the main temple and people came and consulted her and she would make prophesies and answer their questions."

"That's right," said Aldo. "Well I'm glad someone here seems to know their subject." He glared at the other students. "Her prophesies were made when she was in a semi euphoric state induced by inhalation of the gas ethylene, which is sweet smelling and often occurs associated with volcanic activity. Do you get what I'm driving at?" The students exchanged glances.

"You think that this is another oracle?" said Marco.

"I do, but there's only one way to find out."

"But Roberto wasn't euphoric," said the girl frowning. "He was having some sort of fit."

"Then we must be extra careful. Ethylene, in too high a concentration, can cause convulsions and death. There are records of at least one priestess meeting such a fate at Delphi."

"But shouldn't we wait to get gas masks then?" said Marco.

"And shouldn't we try to find Roberto first?" said the girl.

Aldo paused. They were right, of course. But if the worst had happened and Roberto was dead, they would shut down the dig. This was the discovery of a lifetime. He had been waiting sixty years for something like this, something that would make his name live on, and as the years encroached he had felt this need more keenly. He had no children to remember him, but with a discovery like this his name would never be forgotten. There was no time to wait for gas masks. It had to be now. He turned to Marco.

"Bring the camera, I want this on record. And stay close. We'll smell the gas before it can affect us too badly. And be careful." He paused and glanced round at the students. "And you lot had better start looking for Roberto."

Taking the torch from Marco, Aldo started down the steps. Marco hesitated a moment and then followed.

Close up he could see the carvings in much more detail and he passed the torchlight slowly over the intricate figures. The workmanship was exquisite.

"It's old, isn't it? Pre Roman," said Marco behind him, operating the camera.

Aldo nodded. "Very old. I think it's Etruscan – the style of the figures is typical, and yet different. Certainly an Etruscan influence though."

"Etruscans? I thought they were further north."

"There are some indications that their influence extended this far south, and there could be some Greek influence here too. It's hard to tell." He continued on down the stairs, noticing how worn they were, how many feet had passed this way. The oracle must have been in operation for a long time. So it was strange that there were no records of it. He shone his light on the walls and studied the images. More figures, dancing, embracing, images of ancient ceremonies, perhaps ceremonies held in this very temple. He breathed in slowly through his nose. No gas so far. He continued down.

And then the images changed.

Aldo stopped and behind him Marco shifted his feet, scuffing on the stone.

"I don't like these pictures," Marco said. Aldo passed the light over them. The figures were now contorted, writhing in agony, weeping, screaming. They were scenes of murder, dismemberment and death before a backdrop of wild beasts and swirling patterns.

"The effects of the gas," Aldo suggested. "Some ceremonial frenzy, or maybe sacrifices to their gods. Perhaps this was how this oracle worked. This is interesting stuff. I've not heard of anything like it anywhere else. And look at these wonderful mythological creatures. Superb! Come on Marco. Stop shaking." He hurried down the next few steps. "Ah, writing!"

He felt Marco's breath behind him and could hear the faint whirr of the camera in the silence of the chasm. He swept the beam of light backwards and forwards across the script.

"Odd. This isn't Etruscan, or Greek, or any language I've ever come across," he muttered. "This is something new."

"I think I can smell gas," said Marco, and Aldo could detect a quavering in his voice. He ignored him.

"And look at this, it appears to be some sort of map." He scanned the shapes carved into the rock face. It was a map of the skies, constellations but with the stars slightly out of position to their location in the sky that he knew. He smiled. "This must be the night sky as it was when this temple was built," he said, his heart starting to race with excitement. "We can use it to date this thing."

"I really can smell gas," said Marco lowering the camera. Aldo glared at him.

"Don't stop filming! This is amazing! This is the discovery of a lifetime! Look at this star here, larger than the others."

"That's Castor," said Marco. "Slightly out of position." Aldo raised his eyebrows. "Astronomy's a hobby of mine," he added.

Aldo shone the light down into the darkness. For a moment he thought he saw something move in the shadows but when he shone his light towards it there was nothing there. But it did look as if the steps opened out into some sort of chamber below. He started forwards.

"We've got to go back now, the gas," said Marco behind him.

"I thought I saw something move."

"It's the gas or the devil. I told you. We have to go!"

Aldo paused. There was indeed a strange sweet scent in the air.

"Come on," said Marco.

But now Aldo could see movement up ahead, and this time it did not vanish in the light of his torch beam: the figure of a man, face hidden in shadow. Behind he vaguely heard a clatter of footsteps and he knew that Marco was leaving him. But it didn't matter.

He reached the bottom of the steps and now he could see the size and shape of the chamber. It appeared to be hewn out of the native rock and formed a perfect dome, and he marvelled at the skill of the craftsmen who had built such a shrine. The scent was stronger now and stung the back of his throat, but his mind felt clear. He stepped towards the figure. Somewhere in the back of his mind he knew that he ought to leave.

"I must be hallucinating," he thought, and wondered why he had never heard about ethylene gas producing this sort of effect before.

And then the figure was behind him following him down the steps and Aldo turned and gasped and his chest felt tight, for the man staring back at him was himself. At first he thought their eyes had met, but then he realized that the figure was staring past him, at something beyond. And then the figure stumbled and fell, rolling down the last few steps. For a moment it seemed that the sun was shining and the steps the figure had fallen on were made of marble. Aldo saw his head smash against the stone. There was no sound but he could see the splinters of bone and the oozing blood that spread into a dark stain. The mouth gaped once as the staring eyes gave up their fire. Aldo felt his vision darken and the world began to spin around him. He felt that he was falling and in the distance he could hear a whirring noise like machinery starting up. Then he felt strong hands holding him, lifting him, as he drifted into the void.

Aldo wiped the sweat from his forehead with his handkerchief, then replaced his hat. He had thought he had fully recovered from the effects of gas inhalation the previous day but the climb was making him feel dizzy. He squinted against the glare of the sun, his chest heaving with the exertion. The students were dotted around the site, digging, the sun beating down on them. Dust covered their limbs and clothes making them look like grey wraiths. In the distance he could hear the drumming beat of a helicopter's rotors echoing from the rocky buttresses as it searched the mountainside. They still hadn't found Roberto.

Marco was waiting for him by the entrance to the oracle. He was kneeling, adjusting some black tubing that he had attached to a couple of metal cylinders. He glanced up as he heard Aldo approaching over the rough terrain, loose pumice sliding beneath his shoes. The entrance to the cavern was taped off and a large sign stating 'DANGER No Entry' had been placed in front of it. Aldo frowned as he looked at it.

Marco stood up and smiled.

"Feeling better?" he asked. Aldo nodded. The effects of the gas had been unsettling. He hadn't expected to hallucinate. He glanced down at the equipment Marco was assembling.

"What's all this then?"

Marco grinned, flashing his teeth like a wolf. "My brother runs a scuba diving school down the coast. I borrowed these pony cylinders off him."

Aldo nodded. "So we're going back down?"

"Yes. I want to show you something, while we still can. If they find Roberto…" He didn't finish the sentence but Aldo knew what he was thinking. The diving gear was a good idea.

"And here was I thinking you were going to show me the casts," he said.

Marco laughed as he lifted one of the cylinders and adjusted the straps on Aldo's shoulders, then handed him a torch. "I think we're going to find them a disappointment," he said. "They took much more plaster than I had expected. It's going to take another couple of days to dry but I think it's probably just a natural void."

"Shame," said Aldo. "I hoped we'd have some bodies." He put in the mouthpiece and took a couple of deep breaths, listening to the valve hissing as he inhaled and tasting the cold air from the cylinder. He removed it and smiled at Marco. "Works well."

Marco shouldered his cylinder and picked up his torch.

"Warn us if anyone comes," he said to the female student who was pretending to work nearby, scraping at the dusty earth with a trowel. She glanced up at Marco and smiled in response, and Aldo could see something in her eyes as she looked at him that suggested that they were more than just mere colleagues. He hadn't noticed it before.

Marco led the way down into the dark, his footsteps confident, none of the fear he had shown the day before.

"You've been back here, haven't you," said Aldo as he followed him down, smelling the dampness of the cool air and hearing his footsteps echoing in the void below. They weren't using the compressed air just yet. Not until they started to smell the gas.

"Yes," said Marco without looking round. "I wasn't sure at first. I had to come back. The breathing gear helped. But it wasn't the same."

"What do you mean?"

Marco paused a moment allowing the beam of his torch to pan across the walls. Aldo saw the same scenes of death and dismemberment that he remembered from his first visit.

"Do you remember a noise? Like a whirr of machinery?"

Aldo paused. "I thought I heard something. But I was hallucinating. I thought I imagined it."

In the dark in front of him Marco stopped and turned. Aldo could see his eyes shining as points of light as the torchlight reflected off the rocky surfaces around them.

"What sort of hallucination?" he asked.

Aldo swallowed and his mouth felt dry. "I'm not really sure," he said, trying to push the images away, trying not to see the silent smashing of bone on marble.

"Did you see your own death?" The intensity on Marco's voice suddenly frightened him. He had seen himself die, but it was after all, just a hallucination induced by gas inhalation. It wasn't real.

"How do you die?" Marco pressed.

"I take it you saw something similar?"

Marco nodded slowly and started down the steps once more. Aldo followed, puzzled. After a few moments Marco started to speak again, and his voice sounded dreamy and distant.

"I saw myself as a very old man, in an airy room with the sunlight drifting in through white curtains and a gentle breeze blowing in the sounds and scents of the sea. I was surrounded by people, Sophia, that girl outside was one, but she was very old then, almost as old as me, and there were younger people standing around, a couple of young men who looked very much as I do now and some women and children. Somehow I knew that they were all my family and I was at peace."

"It's just a hallucination," said Aldo. "Not a premonition."

Marco glanced back up at him his eyes narrow. "You're too much of a sceptic. Why would we both see our own destiny? So how are you going to die? It is peacefully?"

"Superstitious nonsense. It means nothing." Aldo could feel the irritation beginning to crawl beneath his skin. They were passing the star map and approaching the main chamber now. He could smell the faint scent of ethylene and lifted the mouthpiece to his lips. The compressed air tasted slightly metallic but at least his head remained clear this time. The valves hissed as he breathed. Marco stood in the middle of the chamber, scanning the walls with his torch. Aldo allowed his own beam to probe the shadows. He was baffled by what he saw. The chamber was a perfect dome, but the walls were not rock as he had first thought. The dome was entirely artificial. He stared at the smooth surfaces, which looked as if they were made of something halfway between metal and plastic. One wall was glowing dimly as if lit from within. Aldo frowned. This wasn't right.

Marco pointed towards the lights and removed his mouthpiece to speak.

"When we heard that sound those lights came on as well." He was standing beside the dim glow in the cavern wall, replacing his mouthpiece to breathe between sentences. "They weren't there before. But when I came back here on my own and let myself breathe in the gas and watched my own death again, nothing happened."

Aldo removed his own mouthpiece to speak. He could taste the sweet smell of the ethylene gas as he did so.

"So? What are you thinking? What is this place?"

"It's a machine of some kind. That much is obvious. A machine that dates back from before the Romans."

Aldo suppressed the urge to laugh. "The Etruscans weren't technologically advanced like this. It has to be modern."

Marco reached out a hand to touch the wall. Aldo could see the lights glowing red through his skin. Then he turned, his eyes dark pools in the dim light, his shadow wavering on the wall behind him, where it was cast by the beam of Aldo's torch.

"How do you die Aldo? Is it a violent death?"

Aldo shrugged. This was getting silly. There had to be a logical explanation for all of this. But when he thought about what he had seen he couldn't help feeling a creeping unease. "I saw myself fall, but I've told you, it was just gas induced delirium."

"I thought it must be. Remember the carvings we passed on the way down here, the dismemberment and torture."

Aldo hesitated a moment before replying. He shifted his feet. Marco's eyes appeared to have darkened.

"Yes. I take it you have a theory?"

Marco nodded slowly and came over to stand in front of him. Aldo could see beads of sweat of his forehead, glowing like amber tears. He hadn't replaced his mouthpiece.

"They're human sacrifices. Barbaric I know. And the images show them being put to death in a violent manner."

"I thought the same when I saw them."

"Ah, but don't you see…?"

"I think you'd better put your mouthpiece back in Marco, the gas is starting to affect you."

"I can see it now Aldo. I can see the room, and all my family around me. But nothing is happening to the lights."

"I think we'd better leave." Aldo reached out his hand and placed it on Marco's shoulder, but Marco was staring into the distance. His voice sounded dreamy and a long way off.

"You'll see it without the gas. I did. And in any case, whoever heard of ethylene producing this kind of vision? No. This is something else."

Aldo looped his arm around Marco's waist and pulled his hand over his shoulder, then started to pull him towards the steps.

"It was when you saw yourself die in a fall. Your brain released some sort of energy that started up the machine. Imagine how much energy would be released if you saw yourself being brutally murdered and dismembered whilst you were still alive. That's what they were trying to do with those sacrifices!"

Aldo felt a flush of anger pushing away any misgivings. For a moment he had taken Marco's suggestions seriously. But now he had gone too far. He was risking them both behaving like this. As if the hallucinations could have any effect on a machine – if indeed it even was a machine! Marco stumbled slightly, drunk with ethylene gas. His eyes were wide with euphoria.

They reached the bottom of the steps and Aldo's head was starting to swim. He staggered as he forced himself up the first of the steps. Marco was a dead weight, mumbling incoherently about sacrifices and ancient machines. Aldo had never heard such nonsense. He had to admit that it was all a bit of a puzzle though.

Then his vision darkened.

He was puzzled at first. This shouldn't be happening! He was still using the breathing apparatus. The gas shouldn't be affecting him! His head started to swim. And then he saw it. He saw a figure coming down a flight of marble stairs. A cold chill passed through him as he saw himself fall. He saw his head smash and the blood spread as his last breath left his body. He was aware that the sun was shining and that the marble of the steps was red with unusual fossils embedded in it. Behind him he heard a whirr of machinery and he could see an increased glow of lights, that didn't come from his or Marco's torches.

Then someone was calling him in the darkness and he could hear footsteps approaching down the steps. He recognized the voice of the girl student.

"Come quickly," she was calling. "They've found Roberto!"

The images vanished as quickly as they had come, and the girl was beside him, helping him haul Marco out and into the warm fresh air.

Aldo rapped on the door and entered the room. Marco was sitting behind a plain wooden desk tapping at a keyboard and he rose to his feet when he saw Aldo enter. Aldo looked around the office, at the piles of journals and papers and stacked bookcases. The sun was shafting in between the blinds casting long shadows on the stone floor, and the air in the office was pleasantly cool after the sun baked heat of the streets outside. Marco came over and kissed him lightly on both cheeks.

"I'm glad you could come," he said.

"I always like visiting Rome, and it's only right that I should come to pay my last respects to Roberto."

Marco nodded and Aldo could see the sadness in his eyes. They had sealed off the site after they had found the body, cancelled the dig and blocked the cavern with concrete lest anyone should succumb to a similar fate. The gas was too dangerous. Yet there were so many questions still to be answered.

"I thought you ought to see the casts," Marco said.

"Oh. I thought you said they were natural voids. Did you find bodies after all?"

Marco smiled. "Sort of. Follow me."

He led the way along a corridor and into another room. This appeared to be some kind of store, filled with assorted junk, old computers, obsolete equipment and boxes of old journals. The blinds were half closed and the room smelt musty. Marco pulled back a dustsheet and Aldo drew in an involuntary breath as he stared in disbelief.

"What on earth is that?" he gasped.

The plaster cast before him was huge. For a moment he thought that the contorted shape was just some artifact caused by the volcano, but then he realized that he was looking at a creature of some sort, twice the size of a man, with a large lobate head and pendulous arms and legs which ended in long claws. It seemed to have a tail which was twisted back on itself and some sort of ridge along its back. It looked like the mythical creatures they had seen carved on the walls of the oracle. But these beasts before him were no myth. Marco pulled back another dust sheet and there was another one.

"This is crazy," said Aldo. "These things were in the ash?"

Marco slowly replaced the dust sheets and Aldo followed him out of the store room. He locked the door behind them.

"I don't think anyone will ever believe me," Marco said as he walked back along the corridor. "But I think they are the ones that built that machine we found. I think they died in the AD 79 eruption."

"But why? What for?"

Marco smiled.

"Remember that star map? I think they were just trying to get home." He paused at the top of a long flight of marble stairs. "Shall we get some lunch?"

Aldo nodded and started down the stairs, shocked and baffled by what he had just seen, and at the same time excited. He had to try to get the dig re-opened. They had to find out the truth behind all this. This was going to be his moment. This discovery would be his monument. And then he noticed that the marble beneath his feet was red, with unusual fossils embedded in its fabric, and outside the sun was shining – as his foot slipped from beneath him...

THE GREEN MAN

Alec peered ahead through the thin drizzle that the wiper blades were smearing across the windscreen. There was a figure moving in the road up ahead, shadowy in the shrouds of mist; a figure in army uniform, brandishing an assault rifle and signalling for him to stop. He brought his foot down hard on the brake.

The soldier came across and rapped on the driver's side window. Behind him a number of armoured vehicles blocked the road and more armed figures were moving through the fine rain like ghosts in mist. He wound down his window and looked into the man's cold eyes.

"Turn around and go back," the soldier said, his accent coarse, his breath stale.

"But why?"

"Go back the way you came."

"But I'm trying to get to..."

"Go back. There's no way through for you. Nobody goes any further than here. And don't try going around. All the roads heading west are blocked." The soldier stepped back from the car and gestured with his gun for Alec to turn about and leave. Alec hesitated. Through the drifting curtains of fine rain he could see a group of figures disembarking from a jeep. They all appeared to be wearing some kind of radiation or chemical suits. Then the soldier took a step towards him once more and Alec hastily put the car into reverse.

He puzzled over it as he drove away. The soldier had said not to try to find another way through. But why would that be? He passed a television van, parked in a lay-by, yet the DJ on the radio was still chattering away aimlessly. There was no hint of any major news story. Something wasn't right.

He pulled over by the side of the road, listening to the beat of the wiper blades sweeping back and forth and the inane chatter from the radio. He had promised Rachel he would join her at her brother's place. And he wasn't about to break his promise. There was something about her. He had felt it the instant he took his seat next to her on the aeroplane. Sometimes you just knew about someone.

Alec tightened his grip on the steering wheel. He was going to keep his promise. He reached for the map that was lying on the seat beside him and started to study it in detail. He still had over a hundred miles to go, but he was in a Range Rover, and if he went off road he might just be able to get past the soldiers. He put down the map and shifted the car into gear.

After a good hour of driving along dirt tracks and green lanes Alec decided he could brave the minor roads. He passed a few houses but they seemed to be deserted. Livestock were standing idle in the fields and a cat darted across the road in front of him. But he didn't see another human being.

And then, cresting the brow of a hill, the landscape changed. Alec stopped the car and stared out at the scene before him. Up until now he had been driving past lush fields and woodlands, but ahead of him everything was brown and dead, as if the whole landscape had been scorched or sprayed with weed killer. He could see where it all changed, a few dozen yards up ahead, abruptly, like a sharp line drawn in ash. Outside the rain began to intensify, as if the very landscape itself was weeping. Alec shuddered and tried to suppress the creeping feeling of unease. Rachel was out there somewhere. He drove on, through piles of leaves that had fallen from the trees that lined the road, and yet it was spring. The dead hedges and fields glistened in the rain.

Following the directions Rachel had given him he came at last to St Petroc's. But rather than the quaint English church he had expected to see there was just a ruin. He climbed out of his car, pulling his coat close against the penetrating rain, and pushed open the wooden gate, slimy and wet beneath his hands, wrinkling his nose at the acrid smell of sodden ash, and an odd chemical smell that seemed to underlie everything else. There was no sound other than the sound of the rain, dripping from the dead branches. All that remained of the church was parts of the walls, soot scorched black, and Alec's nose told him that this fire had been recent.

Rachel paused, her hand on the old wooden gate, rough with lichen, and looked across the graveyard towards the church. It was very old, typically Norman, built of the local granite, a grey church beneath a blue sky, with the open moor stretching away beyond towards the craggy outcrop of Glass Tor.

The churchyard smelled of freshly mown grass. There were daffodils flowering on some of the graves and in the surrounding hedges, and skylarks were calling above. The gargoyles leered at her from the tower and the weather-beaten statue of Saint Petroc above the oak door had half his face missing. But the door itself was open and she could see someone moving in the shadows inside. She guessed that it must be her brother, and sweeping a stray strand of blonde hair from her face, she pushed open the gate and headed along the path, past the war memorial towards him.

He glanced up at the sound of her footsteps. A flicker of recognition passed across his face and then he frowned. Rachel hesitated, suddenly unsure of her welcome. It had been over a year and she hadn't warned him that she was coming. But then she saw the bucket by his feet, the cloth in his hand, and the red paint graffiti on the oak door.

"Hello Dan," she said. "Trouble with vandals?"

Daniel turned back towards the defacing paint and mopped slowly at the writing. The paint smeared across the wood like the blood of a martyr. She shifted her feet. He was wearing jeans, as she was, but the white dog collar marked his vocation.

"The gardener at the rectory said I'd find you up here," she said. Daniel nodded but didn't reply. "I'm sorry I didn't call and warn you I was coming. I lost my phone and…"

Daniel dropped the cloth back into the bucket and turned towards her. This time he was smiling. Rachel felt a surge of relief.

"I'm sorry. I'm being rude. You just caught me at a bad time." He nodded towards the door.

"I can see. Who did this?"

Daniel shrugged. "Local kids. Not a lot to do around here and no respect." There was a hint of suppressed anger in his voice.

"I'll help you if you like."

Daniel's smile cracked open wider to show a flash of white teeth.

"It's really good to see you Rachel," he said.

# #

The paint removed and the door returned to plain wood and brass, Rachel was able to take her first good look around St. Petroc's while Daniel tidied away the bucket and cloths. It was a particularly fine church, oak pews, black with age, the pew ends ornately carved, and stained glass windows depicting biblical scenes in vivid colours as the sunlight shafted through to cast rainbow patterns on the stone floor. Around the walls the Stations of the Cross were carved in wood and there were a number of memorial plaques inscribed in Latin. But it was the scene above the altar that caught her eye.

At first glance it appeared to be a fairly typical stained glass crucifixion scene, fine workmanship and vivid colours, but as she studied it in more detail she began to notice something familiar about the landscape in the background. She tipped her head to one side as she puzzled over it. And there was something strange about the way the scene was bordered with intertwining leaves. Footsteps sounded in the aisle behind her and she half turned her head as Daniel joined her, wiping his hands on his shirt.

"Admiring our windows?" he said.

Rachel nodded.

"There's something about the background…"

Daniel laughed. "You saw it as you came into the churchyard. It's Glass Tor."

"So it is. How strange."

"Not really. Glass Tor is at the centre of the moor. It's a special place to the locals. These windows are very old. I guess the people who made them thought it fitting."

Rachel tipped her head again and squinted her eyes. The sun had moved round slightly and was starting to shine through the window and dazzle her, but it also had the effect of highlighting the border.

"There's a face in the leaves," she said. She glanced at Daniel, then back to the window.

"That's the Green Man," he said.

"The Green Man?" The more she stared the more faces she could see, shadowy faces made up entirely of leaves, mouths open, eyes hollow, hair streaming fronds. She gave an involuntary shudder.

"They look like they're screaming," she said in a whisper.

"It's quite a common image in churches this age."

She turned quickly towards him. "It is?"

Daniel was smiling. "Yes. Particularly in this part of the country, but it's a very widespread image. You find green men all over Britain, right across Europe and as far away as India. But there's a particularly high concentration of them in the churches on this moor."

"Really?"

"Yes. Here in St. Petroc's I've counted forty-nine green men. Just look at these ones on the bench ends." He stroked the age-blackened wood and she followed his gaze, giving a short gasp of surprise as she realised that the intricate carving she had noticed earlier did in fact form the shape of a face, another green man. But this face, rather than being made up of leaves like the faces in the window above the altar, was more skull like, and the leafy fronts were growing outwards from its mouth and from its eye sockets and where the ears would be to stream with the foliage hair around the bench end. And there was another on the next pew, and the next.

"They're hideous," she whispered. "What do they mean?"

"They're just symbolic."

"Not very Christian."

Daniel grinned. "No. They're much older than Christianity. Nobody really knows much about them. Some think they are some sort of ancient fertility god, others that they represent life after death, like these bench ends, new growth coming from the dead, hence the skulls. But nobody really knows. Whatever their true meaning was has been lost to us over the ages."

"Fascinating," said Rachel. The face before her stared back from empty eye sockets and she couldn't dispel the thought that it was screaming. "I've never come across them before."

Daniel laughed. "Well now you'll be seeing them all over the place. There's a book about the churches around here back at the Rectory. It won't tell you much but I'll show you anyway."

Rachel nodded.

"And I bet you're hungry."

She nodded again.

"Well, how about some lunch, and you can tell me all about what you've been up to this past year." Rachel drew a deep breath and smiled. She hoped he wouldn't mind when she told him about Alec.

Rachel sat on the leather sofa, her feet tucked up beneath her, watching the flames lapping at the log Dan had just placed on the fire. The wood was fresh and the sap was boiling out of one end. Dan ran his fingers along the spines of the books that lined the opposite wall.

"Are you sure it's all right?" she said.

Dan didn't look round, but continued his search.

"Of course. You've just invited some strange bloke you met on the plane to come and stay at my house. Why should I mind?" But Rachel could see that he was smiling.

She glanced out of the window, pulling her jumper close. The sun was still fairly high but there was a chill in the air despite the fire. She could just make out the roof of St Petroc's and Glass Tor looming purple behind it.

"Ah, here it is."

She looked round. Daniel pulled one of the volumes from the shelf and smiled as he joined her on the sofa. The book in his hands was old and leather bound. She could see its title embossed in gold on the cover.

"'*The Green Men of Glass Tor*'," she read out loud.

Daniel flipped through the first few pages.

"It was written by a predecessor of mine back in the late eighteen hundreds. Some of the ideas are pretty strange. I don't think he was quite all there."

"Let's see..."Rachel took the book from him and scanned the pages. "Most of this seems to be about architecture." There was disappointment in her voice, although she had no idea what she had expected to find.

"Yes but look at this map." Daniel turned to the middle of the book.

Rachel stared at the map. It depicted the moor. The villages and churches were boldly marked.

"The churches are all lined up in a circle," she said. "With Glass Tor in the middle. Is that right?" she glanced up at her brother. He nodded.

"Yes. It's right, uncannily so in fact. I've checked them out on an Ordnance Survey map. The thirteen churches shown do indeed form a perfect circle, with Glass Tor at its centre. And what's even more interesting, all these churches are built on the sites of prehistoric earthworks, ancient temples, or henges."

"Like Stonehenge?"

Daniel laughed. "Yes, but not as impressive. And they're not here anymore. Just the churches."

"Is that usual?"

"Oh yes. It's quite common to build churches on sites that were already sacred. Matey here however," he patted the book where it lay open on Rachel's lap, "had a different theory." He turned over a few more pages and pointed to the text. "There you go."

Rachel began to read.

> *" That the thirteen churches form a perfect circle*
> *around Glass Tor, and that the tor itself is a*
> *geological anomaly only adds to the conundrum. "*

She paused, looking up at Dan. "Geological anomaly?"

He nodded.

"Yes, indeed. And in fact Glass Tor is really something of a puzzle."

"Oh?"

"There was a geology professor staying in the village a while back who was studying the thing. He took a load of samples off for analysis and wrote to me some time later with his results. But his results only made the puzzle deeper."

Dan paused and ran one hand through his hair.

"Go on," said Rachel.

"Well the whole moor is made up of the same rock type, apart from Glass Tor. Most of the moor is granite. Apparently it's a huge batholith that was emplaced at depth and cooled very slowly, hence the large crystals that make the rock so characteristic. Glass Tor, however, is formed of obsidian."

"That's that black glassy stuff isn't it?"

"Yes," Dan smiled.

"So why is that so strange?"

Daniel paused and looked at her. There was an odd expression in his eyes that she couldn't quite fathom.

"The professor did a chemical analysis of the rocks. He found that the granite and the obsidian are chemically identical. He also managed to date the obsidian. It's only three thousand years old."

Rachel stared at her brother.

"But that's ridiculous!" she gasped.

"I know. It sounds crazy. But the Professor concluded that something must have melted that portion of the moor. And I'll tell you something else that's strange. The henges that were here before the churches – they're three thousand years old too."

Rachel sat in silence, trying to absorb what Dan had just said. For some reason she had the feeling that it was important, although she couldn't think why that should be. The log on the fire settled with a shower of orange sparks. Dan rose to his feet and walked over to the window, staring out at Saint Petroc's hands clasped behind his back. The sun was beginning to dip towards the west and a few high level clouds were smeared across the sky. She ran her hands over the coarse paper of the book and turned the pages one by one.

"So this Alec. You really like him don't you?"

Rachel glanced up at Dan. He still had his back to her.

"It's weird. I've only just met him, but it's as if I know. It's as if it's meant to be."

"Well, I can't wait to meet him."

"I know you're going to get on." Rachel lifted the book from her lap, intending to put it down and join Dan by the window, but as she did so she noticed the picture on the page she had just turned. She hesitated.

"Oh look, another green man!"

"You like this little puzzle don't you?" said Dan.

Rachel glanced at the text beneath the picture, then laughed.

"Listen to this:

" Ergo it is obvious to conclude that Glass Tor is inexorably linked to the Green Man image... The circle must not be broken. "

"I see what you mean about him being a bit crazy. What nonsense!"

She looked up at Dan, but was surprised to see that he wasn't smiling. His brow was furrowed into a frown and he looked serious. Behind him the sinking sun was lighting up the clouds in purple and gold and a grey mist was obscuring the church and the tor from view.

"There are people around here who don't believe the Green Man to be merely symbolic," he said slowly.

Rachel scowled as she looked at him. For a moment he sounded as if he believed such stuff. And then she noticed that the grey mist that shrouded St Petroc's was billowing up into the sky, and beneath she could see the flicker of orange light in the gathering gloom. She gasped.

"Daniel! The church!" She jumped to her feet and dashed to the window as Dan turned to look out. St Petroc's was ablaze, flames flickering across the slate roof, smoke drifting away with the wind. Beside her Daniel drew in a sharp breath.

"My church!" he gasped. And then he turned and was running out from the house. Rachel followed, shoving her feet into her trainers and grabbing her coat as she raced after him, out into the chill spring air, and up the lane towards the burning church.

They reached St Petroc's as the first of the fire tenders arrived, sirens screaming up the lane with a flash of blue lights. The police were already there and she heard the word 'arson' muttered in the gloom. Daniel stood apart from the clusters of spectators who had gathered nearby, and his face was ashen. Across the churchyard she could see a small group of teenage boys, hoods pulled over their heads, lurking by the hedge. They melted away into shadows as the police approached.

A dull thud that she felt, rather that heard, drew her attention back to the fire and was followed by a crash of breaking glass, shards scattering across the graves as the first of the stained glass windows exploded. Something ached inside her as she thought of those beautiful windows and their intricate designs, now lost for ever. Flames were leaping from the roof and the police began to move people back as the firemen unreeled their hoses and arcs of water began to play across the fire. She realised that she was standing next to Daniel once more, and the pain showed clearly on his face as he watched the destruction of his church.

"The circle must not be broken," he muttered under his breath.

"What?" said Rachel. But in that instant the roof of St Petroc's collapsed in a shower of glowing sparks, and half of the tower and the west wall went with it. Tears were glistening, darts of orange light, in the corners of Daniel's eyes and as she watched a single tear, reflecting amber, rolled down his cheek.

"The circle hasn't been broken for three thousand years," he said. "Until now."

And then the ground shook.

Rachel turned, and beyond the ruined church she could see Glass Tor. But the tor had changed. It was as if it had been ripped open, and an ominous cloud of black smoke, dwarfing the one over the flaming church, was spewing out from its very heart.

The silence of the crowd turned to agitated muttering, as the water from the hoses hissed against the dying flames of the fire. But St Petroc's was now an empty shell, a ruin, and the black smoke from Glass Tor swept rapidly across the heather towards them.

She stared in horror at the oncoming cloud. "What is it?"

Dan was as unnerved as she was. "I've no idea, but it's coming from Glass Tor. I think we're about to find out what the Green Man really means."

And now the cloud was almost upon them. But it wasn't a cloud, it was made of small particles, like flakes of black driven snow, a blizzard of darkness.

"I think it's spores," said Dan. "Shut your eyes."

Rachel did so. She could feel them landing in her hair, and drifting against her skin with a soft caress. And then she heard the screams begin. She clenched her eyes tight, and swallowed hard. They tickled the inside of her nostrils. Then they were in her mouth, popping against her tongue, and they started to hurt. Daniel cried out in pain. She opened her eyes and gasped in horror.

Around the graveyard people were staggering, screaming, clawing at their faces, and beside her Daniel had fallen to his knees. Green tendrils were twisting through his hair, and blood was running from his eyes and nose. And more of the green tendrils were growing there, rupturing his eyeballs, growing outwards from his nose and mouth, to intertwine themselves with those that now formed his hair.

Rachel choked back a scream.

And now there was something moving in her mouth and eyes, and her sight was failing and the pain that had started as just a dull ache intensified.

"Daniel!" she cried out as darkness enveloped her. But he didn't reply. They were growing, covering her face, and she knew that there was nothing anyone could do. This was the curse that those Iron Age priests had found a way to control, had sealed within solid rock long ago, within Glass Tor. The temples that they built, the henges, had been superseded by the churches that stood here now. But their wisdom had been lost in the darkness of time.

Perhaps the spores of these parasitic plants had drifted in from another world, or maybe they had simply evolved here. Whatever their origin, they were free... and this time, nobody would be able to curb their spread.

"Alec," she gasped as she dropped to the ground.

Alec bent down to look closer at the shrivelled grasses. He thought of the soldiers he had seen at the roadblock in their chemical suits and he shuddered. Beyond the ruins he could see the distant shadow of a jagged hill that looked as if it had been torn apart. He could hear nothing but the rain getting heavier as he stood, alone. And suddenly, in the same way that he had realised on that plane, that Rachel was the girl for him, he saw now that whatever had happened here had changed all that. He knew he would never see her again. Tears burned at the back of his eyes and he felt empty, as if his chest was suddenly hollow.

He turned and started walking through the rain back towards his car but then he stopped. There was a fragment of plant near the gate that was still faintly green. He stooped to touch it and as his fingers brushed its surface a few black spores drifted into the air and wafted towards him.

GRIMSTONE MIRE

Kieran Patterson unhooked his water bottle from the side of his rucksack and was about to raise it to his lips, when he noticed the man. He paused and stared, narrowing his eyes, at first not sure of what he was looking at, for the man was barely moving, crouching on all fours, staring at the ground.

The figure didn't move as Kieran approached and he was able to study him in detail; the ill-fitting clothes, rolled up jeans and loose green jacket, the wiry grey hair that tumbled like a mane onto the nape of his neck and the angular features.

"Hello," he said, as he drew near and the man glanced up at him, with deep blue eyes that seemed to know more than they let on.

"Come, look at this," said the man, returning to his scrutiny of the ground before him. Kieran paused, then letting his rucksack fall onto the heather, he squatted down beside him.

"What am I looking at?"

The man smiled and his canine teeth were sharp, like those of a wolf. He pointed at the ground.

"There, aren't they beautiful." In front of him was a clump of tiny reddish-coloured plants. Kieran placed his hands on the damp moss and leaned forwards.

"Sundews," said the man. "Watch how they catch their prey. See that beetle. It doesn't know that it's walking into a trap. The plant is waiting, patient like all carnivorous plants. See now, how the beetle is lured in by the sweet scent of those honey beads. And now he is trapped, struggling in the sweetness. Watch how the plant folds itself in onto its prey. The beetle stops moving, and the plant can digest him slowly."

Kieran shuddered. There was something unnerving about the way the tiny plant trapped its prey. Or was it the thrill in the stranger's voice as he had watched the beetle die? He pushed himself back to squat on his heels and studied the man in more detail, noticing the blue shadow of tattoos on the backs of his hands and rising from beneath his collar onto his neck, and the cheap-looking, obviously fake Rolex watch just visible beneath his coat sleeve.

"Are you a botanist?" he asked.

The stranger smiled but didn't look up. "You could say that. Yes. I guess I am a bit of a botanist."

"Do you spend a lot of time here, studying these plants?"

"In Grimstone Mire? Yes, I come here when I can. And plants? They fascinate me, especially these sundews. That something so tiny can be so deadly."

Kieran frowned. Somehow the tattoos and fake Rolex didn't fit with a botanist. But who was he to judge? He shrugged and rose to his feet, lifting his rucksack.

"I'd never have spotted those. Cheers," he said, but the man did not reply, his attention focused only on the small red plants. Kieran glanced back once as he headed along the track towards the farm, but the man hadn't moved.

# #

Kieran tapped the last tent peg into the soft ground and straightened up, flexing his fingers against the handle of his wooden mallet. He could see the farmhouse, grey granite beneath a thatched roof and the door was now open, a white car parked in the drive. Kieran scowled. That was a police car.

There was another vehicle as well, one that hadn't been here when he started pitching his tent. He had heard it pull up, and the chatter of female voices; a jauntily painted orange and white Volkswagen camper van, its smooth lines disrupted by the surfboards strapped to its roof. They were a long way from the sea.

And then he noticed the girl.

She was leaning against the dry stone wall, not far from his tent, her fair hair tied in two loose braids, her jeans rolled up to just below her knees. She smiled as he caught her eye.

"Hello."

He could hear the twang of her Australian accent as she spoke.

"Hi. What's the surf like?"

She laughed. "Pretty crap around here. Hopefully it'll be a bit better when we get to Newquay."

"That where you're headed?"

She nodded. "Eventually. Touring around a bit first."

"So what do you think of the moor?"

"I like it, it's wild and empty."

Kieran put down the mallet and moved round to the other side of the tent towards her. "What's your name?" he asked.

"Sally." She nodded towards the farmhouse. "And this is Marie."

Kieran turned to see another girl running towards them over the tussocky grass, her brown hair cut in a bob, light cotton dress flapping round her knees. Behind her the policeman was driving slowly away down the lane. His blue light started to flash but he didn't start up his siren.

Marie ran up to them and paused, leaning forwards, her hands on her knees, panting.

"Guess what," she said as soon as she had caught her breath. Kieran noticed with some surprise that her accent was local. He had assumed she would be another Australian. "They've found a body!"

Sally's eyes opened wide with surprise. "Is that why the police car was here?"

"No." Marie straightened up and hooked her hair behind her ears. Then she laughed. "He didn't actually say what he was here about. The call came through while we were talking. But it's not a modern body. It's one of those bog bodies. They found it where they're cutting into the peat to make an access road to the prison through Grimstone Mire." She pointed out towards the moor, and if he peered into the distance Kieran thought he could just make out movement, and a straight scar cut into the heath. "Come on," said Marie. "If we go over the moor we can get there before the police car."

She turned and started back across the field towards the gate that led out onto the moor. Kieran glanced at Sally and she shrugged.

"You pommies," she muttered.

Marie was sitting on the gate waiting for them. As they joined her she dropped down onto the track on the other side. Kieran unfastened the coarse twine that was looped over the gatepost and held the gate open for Sally, closing it securely behind them.

"I've never seen one of these bog bodies," Marie said as they started off along the track. Kieran could feel the peaty earth springy beneath his boots and he glanced at Marie as she walked. She seemed to belong to this place. The wind played with her hair and whipped at the flimsy cotton of her dress. He could see the slender figure hinted at beneath the fabric. Her smile was wide and her teeth flashed white.

"Do you get a lot of them, then?" Sally trotted a short distance to keep up with them, for Marie was walking swiftly over the uneven ground.

"This is the first one I've heard of on this moor." Marie half turned her head, and Kieran was aware of her brown eyes as they lingered and felt himself start to blush. "They've found quite a few in Ireland."

"So what are they?"

Marie's eyes flashed and she replied in a hiss: "Ancient human sacrifices!"

"What? In a bog?"

"Yes. And the bog has preserved them for thousands of years. I can't wait to see it! They're meant to be all brown and shrivelled and... hello, what's this?"

Marie paused and stooped down, almost causing Kieran to blunder into her. When she straightened up she was holding a small notebook. She flicked it open.

"Oh, this is pretty."

Kieran peered over her shoulder. There was a picture on the page in front of her: a pencil drawing, skilfully done, and he recognised the plants in the picture, drawn in minute detail, even down to the dying beetle trapped amongst the sticky honey beads.

"That's a sundew," he said.

Marie turned the page.

"More plants." she started to walk once more. Kieran kept pace beside her. She had left the path now and was walking through the heather, taking long strides through the purple scrub.

"It must belong to that botanist I met," said Kieran.

Marie glanced at him, then turned her attention back to picking her way across the moor.

"What botanist?" said Sally, jogging again to keep up. Kieran could feel the ground getting softer under his feet and it was starting to squelch where his boots landed.

"Strange old boy I met earlier. He had a bit of a thing for these sundews." He decided not to mention the way the man had relished watching that dying beetle.

Marie flicked through the pages of the book. "Botanist, you reckon? Is that what he told you?"

"Well, not exactly."

"There's a map in here of Grimstone Mire." Marie held the book up for him to see.

"Grimstone Mire? That's where we are now."

"And another map on the next page?"

"Well I suppose he's interested in the bog plants."

Marie laughed and handed him the book. "And the next page."

"Maybe it's a botanical map."

"An interest in bog plants or something a bit more sinister perhaps?" said Marie flashing her eyes at him.

Sally stopped in her tracks.

"What do you mean, Marie?"

When Kieran stopped he could feel his feet start to sink into the soft sphagnum moss. The vegetation had changed, heather giving way to marsh grass, bracken to moss.

"We're nearly at the cutting," said Marie, her long legs striding, finding her way with ease. Kieran followed her tracks.

"So where do you suppose this 'botanist' lives?" she said with a flick of her hair. Kieran shrugged.

"You're the local."

Marie laughed. "Not that local. I'm an Ashburton girl. But I know enough about the local colour."

A gentle mist was rising from the marsh as the sun was sinking slowly towards the hills and tors. Kieran could feel the chill and dampness in the air, but ahead he could see the cutting equipment, and cluster of people. The police car was already there but Kieran couldn't tell which was the officer.

"So it didn't occur to you that he might have been residing at her Majesty's pleasure?" said Marie.

"Her Majesty's what?" said Sally, slipping on the wet ground. The mist was swirling around their feet and Kieran almost lost his footing as well.

"She's talking about Dartmoor prison," he explained. "An escaped criminal, in other words."

"Oh... OH!" Sally stopped.

Marie nodded. "Come on. We're nearly there." She gestured towards the figures, now shrouded in a light mist and seeming further away than when Kieran had last looked. A shiver passed down his spine.

"What sort of criminal?" Sally asked, picking her way slowly forwards, glancing around as she walked. There were pools of water on either side of them now, tinged black with peat, and he heard the bog sigh as a bubble of methane gas crept to the surface through the rotting vegetation. He hoped Marie knew where she was taking them.

"Multiple murderer," hissed Marie, leaning towards her and grinning broadly. "You'd better watch out: he'll be coming for you through the mist."

"That's not funny, Marie."

But Marie just laughed and started walking towards the cutting. She glanced back at them as she walked.

"If it really is him they'll pick him up soon enough. He never goes further than Grimstone Mire. He keeps returning to the scene of his crime."

"And what exactly was his crime?" Kieran called after her.

Marie laughed, her voice lost in the mist that was starting to swirl around her.

"Some walkers went missing on the moor. He was always mooching around the bog, so it had to be him. He's broken out before, but never leaves the bog."

Kieran held back and took hold of Sally's hand. She glanced up at him and frowned.

"I don't like this bog," she said.

"It's OK, just watch your footing, these pools of water are deep. Maybe we should have gone round by the road instead."

"Maybe we shouldn't be here at all, chasing after some prehistoric corpse, with some weirdo creeping around in the fog!"

Kieran smiled. "Don't worry. If this guy really is dangerous they'd be making much more fuss than they seem to be. After all, that policeman seems to find this bog body far more interesting."

Sally's grip on his hand eased slightly, but she didn't let go. He could hardly see Marie now, for the mist had thickened and the sun was just a sickly yellow orb, half hidden in vapour. He could smell the stench of the bog rising around them: a smell of decay, of rotten vegetation. The wet ground seemed to shift beneath his feet, and the bog sighed again as the fog condensed around them. Dew frosted his clothes and Sally's hair, and when he looked again he could no longer see Marie. He swallowed, disorientated, and could only guess at the direction to take. Sally's hand was cold in his clasp.

After a few moments he was sure he had missed them, and that they were just wandering deeper into the bog. He tightened his clasp on the botanist's notebook. This fog had risen quicker than he had expected. It made sense that an escaped criminal would make a map to help him find his way through the mire. But then he saw figures looming out of the mist, seeming larger and further away through the grey shrouds, and he felt the firmer ground of the half-finished road beneath his feet.

Marie was standing with a group of contractors, gathered around what he guessed was the body. He could see the policeman now, stooping down to take a closer look. Marie looked round as he arrived beside her.

"It's great, isn't it!" she said. "Look how well preserved it is. You can even see the clothes he was wearing."

Kieran peered down at the body. It was stained brown and quite shrivelled. But what struck him most was the way the face was distorted into a grimace, almost as if the body was screaming. It must have been a horrible way to die.

"Some of them were garrotted first," said Marie. Kieran shivered.

"Is that what those marks are on its neck?"

"No they're tattoos. The ancient Britons were big on tattoos."

The policeman stood up, wiping his hands on his trousers.

"I think this is one for the museum, rather than forensics," said one of the contractors. His colleagues laughed, their voiced muffled by the mist and the sounds of dripping water and the breathing of the bog. The ground seemed to shift beneath them.

"What was that?" said Sally.

"It's pretty unstable here," the contractor said. "We've been cutting a drainage ditch and the peat is starting to shrink as it dries. There should have been some engineers along today to check what footings the new road's going to need, but they never turned up."

The ground shifted again and Kieran dropped the notebook. He stooped to pick it up and as he did so he noticed that it had fallen open on another of the convict's maps of Grimstone Mire. But this was more than just a map. It was more like the picture of the sundews on the first page, but instead of a beetle there were people, struggling, trapped in its clinging wetness.

He glanced up and saw that the body was right in front of him, one hand stretching out, clasping, claw like, and from beneath the sleeve was a glint of metal, for this bog body was wearing a fake Rolex watch.

Beneath them the bog drew in another deep breath.

THE TREES

The trees stirred. They stretched their roots, probing into the cool damp soil, and their branches sighed in the breeze, leaves shivering in the moonlight. Woodland creatures, badger, fox, passed by beneath and an owl hooted gently from above. The trees had been here as long as anyone could remember. The trees had been here for a hundred years.

#

The tree-people came. Ed walked into the clearing and dropped his rucksack onto the leaf mould. He flicked his blond dreadlocks out of his eyes and stared around. Fionnula came up beside him.

"This is the place," he announced grandly, and Fionnula smiled at him. She reached out tentatively and touched the bark of one of the trees, smooth and golden. Then she put her arms around the trunk in fond embrace.

"Hello tree," she said.

Ed suppressed an urge to laugh. She was a daft girl, whimsical. He would tire of her soon enough. For now, though, it thrilled him that he had enticed her away from her wealthy professional parents and her boarding school education, to run away with him to save some trees, and to live like a tramp in the woods. He knew how much her folks hated him for this and the thought was delicious.

Others now entered the clearing, a motley assortment of people, mostly unkempt, mostly young. The dropped their bags and burdens onto the damp earth and gazed around at the trees towering above them.

"Is this it?" One of them, a tall bearded man with heavily tattooed arms, turned to Ed. "Is this where the bypass is going to come?"

"No," giggled Fionnula, still hugging her tree, lank mousy hair pressed against golden bark. "Because we're not going to let them. We're going to save these trees."

Ed glanced over towards her. She was humming gently to herself, still embracing the tree and swaying slowly against it in rhythm to her song. He smiled. She was high, still tripping from the night before, which they had spent in a bus shelter, dusty and stinking of urine. You had to get high in a place like that to forget the cold and the grim reality of the city.

He gazed up at the trees, eyes squinting at the sunlight which filtered down between the shimmering leaves. The he turned towards the others. The bearded man was also looking around.

"Odd looking trees," he remarked.

"They're lovely trees!" Fionnula called across, still cuddling bark. The bearded man shrugged.

"No time to waste," said Ed, stepping forwards, demanding their attention, taking charge. "We'll start work now. Build our shelters high up in the branches, and rope walkways between the trees. That way we'll be impregnable. They'll never be able to shift us!" The people nodded in assent and set to work.

The trees stirred. Something was changing. They pressed their roots deep into the soft earth, but the badgers and foxes had fled. Strange creatures were moving in their branches, large blundering creatures. Nails pierced, axes severed. The trees shifted their boughs.

Ed kissed Fionnula and they made love beneath the stars, their passion fuelled with amphetamine. Then they lay, side by side in the long meadow grass, staring at the sky and the moon, rising, full and golden behind the copse.

"A harvest moon," murmured Ed and Fionnula giggled by his side.

"Our trees look so beautiful in the moonlight," she sighed, stretching in the grass and summer flowers. Ed sat up and started searching his pockets for a smoke. He wasn't really in the mood for one of Fionnula's dreamy conversations. She continued: "They're funny looking trees mind. What sort of trees do you suppose they are?"

"How should I know?"

"Oh I guess you wouldn't. You probably don't get many trees on council estates." She giggled again.

Ed tired of her in that instant. He had always known he would. She was a silly and naïve girl, daughter of a wealthy city trader, and the thrill had been the look of hate in her father's eyes as he saw Ed standing there, hand in hand with his precious offspring. He stood up without a word and started walking back towards the copse, leaving her lying amongst the meadow flowers, humming to herself in the moonlight.

She was right about the trees though. They were a bit strange, the golden bark and shimmering leaves which reflected the sunlight with an inner iridescence. Their branches were stirring beneath the stars as he climbed the rope ladder into their treetop shelter; a makeshift construction cobbled together from corrugated iron and wood, both scavenged and stolen.

He hated to admit it, even to himself, but he was much more like Fionnula than she would ever know. He had never set foot on a council estate and had grown up in the countryside. So it was odd that he couldn't identify these trees. He sat down on the stained and threadbare rugs beside the stove, pulled out a piece of wood he had cut from one of the trees and began to whittle with his hunting knife, noticing as he did so the glow of the bark, the hardness of the wood, and the sap seeping like blood over his fingers as he carved. These were indeed strange trees.

After a while Fionnula appeared at the top of the rope ladder, scrambled over to sit beside him and rested her head on his shoulder. He found himself wishing that she would go away. The branches were swaying and the whole shelter was rocking gently back and forth.

"I think there's a storm coming," she murmured. He ignored her and carried on whittling. "It's odd, 'cos there's no clouds. It's a storm without clouds." She smiled to herself, eyes half closed.

"Silly girl," thought Ed.

Then, suddenly, someone screamed; a piercing scream in the night, a cry of sheer terror that ended abruptly, as if at the flick of a switch. Ed dropped his knife and his carving. Fionnula sat bolt upright beside him.

"What was that?" she whispered, eyes wide with alarm. Ed listened intently. There were no more screams but now he could hear a hubbub of voices, shouting in the darkness, and the sound of someone or something crashing through the undergrowth. Ed swore under his breath.

"Bailiffs. That's what. Curse them. I didn't expect them to come so soon – or in the middle of the night!" He rose and moved towards the rickety door. The shelter was swaying more than ever and he reached out a hand to steady himself.

"Oh, bad karma," Fionnula wailed behind him. He paid her no heed and stepped out into the darkness. He peered into the gloomy shadows below. He could hear and see people rushing back and forth. The camp was in commotion. All was chaos. Then something struck him from behind.

The trees stirred. They pressed their roots deep into the moist meadow soil. They stilled their rocking branches, and a new suite of nutrients enriched their sap. A deer paused beneath, nibbled at the long grasses that lapped against the trunks of the trees as waves lap at the shore, and went on its way. The copse was tranquil in the moonlight.

The engineering contractors arrived with the dawn, and with a police escort. The police went on ahead into the wood, but the copse was deserted. The Head Engineer watched as the Inspector walked slowly through the long grass between the trees. There was no-one there. The tree people had gone. He returned to studying his charts and maps, standing some distance from the trees, on an area of rough and muddy ground.

"They've gone," the Inspector announced on his return, his ruddy face creased into a grin. "You can get on with your work." The Head Engineer felt his body relax. This was a relief. They had been expecting trouble from the tree people, for this was the day that work on the bypass was due to begin, the day they were going to fell the trees. But now the police weren't required. They could pack away their riot shields, for the tree people had left of their own accord. They were about to turn and go about their separate tasks, when the Inspector paused.

"Hello. What's this?" he said, stooping, and picked something up from the mud and compost by his feet. He looked at it closely. "It's a wallet!" He flicked it open and quickly inspected the contents, pulling out a single card for a closer look. "Hmm, driving licence: *Edgar Smythe.*"

"Edgar Smythe? Isn't that that MP's son who went missing?" The Head Engineer turned towards the Inspector, intrigued. The story had been all over the papers a few months back.

"Yes indeed. Son of the Tory Minister of Transport. Disappeared from Cambridge just before his law degree finals." The Head Engineer peered over the inspector's shoulder at the picture on the driving licence. A fresh faced young man, smiling and cheerful, blond hair cropped short. No sign of the dreadlocks which he later wore with such pride.

"So I guess he was among the protesters," the Engineer remarked, and laughed briefly at the irony. "Odd he should have left his wallet."

"Probably just dropped it in the rush to leave." The Inspector said with a shrug. The Engineer smiled and glanced around. The churned earth was littered with the debris of human habitation, wood and rope half buried, a sheet or two of corrugated iron, some stained and threadbare rugs, even a makeshift stove and a pair of jeans. "Look at the mess, all the rubbish they've left behind!" He snorted and turned back to consulting the plans and scratched his head. He consulted his plans again.

"Everything OK?" the Inspector asked.

"Come and take a look at these plans." The Head Engineer spread them out over the bonnet of his car and the men leaned forwards to study them. "I don't know who the surveyors were that drew these plans up but, see here, they've got the trees in completely the wrong place."

The Inspector peered closer. "They're not in the way of the new road at all!"

The Engineer sighed and looked round at his men, waiting to start work. "Looks like I'm going to have to tell these fellows they're not needed." He sighed again and glanced towards the copse, branches stirring gently in the breeze on the hillside.

"Odd looking trees," he thought.

A long time ago, after drifting for aeons through the emptiness of space, the spores had finally come to rest on fertile ground. The trees have been here for a hundred years. And these trees can look after themselves.

DOWN TO THE SEA

Max walked slowly into the empty house, smelling the mustiness of old furniture and damp. The door creaked closed behind him and he paused, closing his eyes, remembering these rooms when they had been filled with life and warmth, a bubble of laughter, a crackle of fire in the hearth. He opened them again and the house was cold.

He wandered into the kitchen. There was a cake on a wire rack beside the cooker, the mixing bowl unwashed in the sink. He frowned. The cake would be stale by now. He moved on into the lounge. A fire had been laid in the grate, but never lit, and on the mantelpiece was a photograph. He reached out and took it down. It showed his parents before he was born, laughing together on the beach, the waves lapping at their ankles, ripples frozen in time just as they were. He ran his finger over the contours of the woman's face.

"Why did you do it, Mum?" he breathed.

He could feel the tears prickling behind his eyes and something choking at his chest. Out in the hallway the grandfather clock slowly ticked the minutes away. He would come back tomorrow to sort her things. But for now what he needed was a beer.

He left the cottage, locking the door behind him, and made his way slowly along the sea wall, towards The Moorings Inn. He could smell the salt and seaweed of low tide and see the sand of the cove, pale in the moonlight, and splashes of silvery spray where the waves broke against the jagged rocks of the headland. This had been a good place to grow up, and he felt a sudden pang of guilt. If he had come back more often perhaps this wouldn't have happened.

"Max!"

He paused and turned, as a tall figure hurried across the road and scrambled up with spidery limbs to join him on the sea wall, fair hair and eyes sunken in dark shadow.

"I heard you were back," he said. "I'm so sorry"

Max swept his hand over his wind tugged hair, feeling the salt crust already forming. "I should have come back sooner, Toby. I never realised she was so unhappy."

Toby frowned and his eyes appeared to darken.

"Don't blame yourself," he said. "And besides. There's more."

"More?" Max scowled. What more could there be? An elderly widow, forgotten, alone, decides she's has enough. It was sad, yet simple.

"There have been other…" Toby started to say, but something on the edge of his vision had caught Max's eye, and he turned to look towards the sea. A figure was moving on the edge of the water, arms outstretched and hair flowing long behind her, outlined in sliver by the foam and spume of the waves.

"Who's that?" he said as Toby broke off, mid phrase. The water was already up to the young woman's thighs and still she walked forwards, into the sea, the waves reaching for her like claws, drawing her in.

"What's she doing?" Toby said.

Without thinking Max jumped down from the wall, landing heavily in the damp sand, and then he was running, running into the waves, hearing them roar against the pebbles, feeling the rush of the undertow that sucked on his legs. His shoes were full of salt water and grit and his trousers clung to the skin and hairs of his legs. Then Toby was beside him as he grabbed her arm.

She struggled against him, seeming in a trance, staring out at the horizon.

"No," she gasped. "Let me go." She tried to shake off his grip, but Toby grasped her other arm. She struggled again, then her legs crumpled beneath her.

Together they pulled her from the sea and laid her limp form down on the sand. The waves swept up the beach towards them, as if reaching for their prey, then sank back into darkness.

Max swept her wet dark hair back from her face. She looked so pale in the moonlight, skin like alabaster. Her eyes were closed and her chest heaved gently up and down beneath the cotton of her dress.

"I saw her last night," he said.

Toby looked round at him. "I don't recognise her."

"She was in The Moorings, with a man. I think they're holidaymakers. She recommended the wrasse to me, and she was right." He half licked his lips at the thought, but all he could taste was salt and grit, the taste of fresh fish a half forgotten memory.

"Let's take her up to your Mum's cottage," said Toby. "Warm her up."

# #

With a log spitting in the grate, Max adjusted the fireguard and looked around the room. The firelight and permeating warmth made the place feel more like the home he remembered and he half expected to hear his mother clattering around in the kitchen.

The girl was lying on the sofa, her eyes still closed, her hair starting to dry into matted strands. Toby had finished examining her and was squatting back on his heels.

"She seems perfectly fine," he said. "But there's something odd." He reached for her arm where it lay on top of the blanket he had covered her with, her fingers twitching as if at a distant dream. "Look at these marks."

Max moved closer. Beneath her skin were a series of purplish lines that looked like veins but ran in the wrong direction. Max frowned. "What are they?" he said.

"I don't know, but they're all over her body. But what's bothering me is that the others had them too."

"What others?" said Max.

"The other drownings. That's what I was about to tell you. There's been a spate of drownings in this village over the past few months. They've been keeping it quiet, putting it down to natural causes, after all, in a community like this one, ships are lost and people drown. But I do the post mortems, and all bar one have borne marks such as these."

"My mother?" Max whispered and Toby looked up at him, the shadows beneath his eyes deeper than ever.

"Your mother bore these marks too," he said.

Max felt a shiver pass up his spine as he looked at the girl, lying there, her fingers twitching, her eyes now darting around beneath closed lids. Last night she had been laughing with her boyfriend in the pub, and now this. He shuddered.

"Did you see my mother at all?" he asked, his voice barely more than a whisper. "Before…"

Toby nodded. "Yes. I met her by the bus stop. She seemed perfectly happy. So did the others as far as I can make out."

"Were they all put down to suicides then?"

"Some. Others the inquests came back as accidental death. But I'm beginning to wonder if they weren't suicides at all. Look at this girl." He gestured with his hand at the figure before them. She had stopped twitching and was lying still once more. "You saw her last night. Did she seem the type to kill herself?"

Max shook his head. "No, not at all. She was with her boyfriend. They seemed really happy, recently engaged, very much in love. But then, you never really know. I was sitting at the next table, reading the menu, and she leaned over and suggested I tried the wrasse. So I did. It was excellent."

Toby pulled a face. "I don't like fish, but I've heard the same. It's a particular sort of wrasse they're catching these days."

"Well I don't know why they never caught them before. Tastes much better than cod." Max looked down at the girl. "What should we do about her?"

"Let her sleep I suppose. We can talk to her when she wakes. Try to find out what's wrong."

"You should stay," said Max. "I'm booked in to the Moorings because I didn't think I could bear it here with Mum gone, but with a fire lit, and some company it doesn't seem so bad."

Toby smiled. "That's a fine looking malt on the shelf behind you," he said.

Max woke as the first grey light of dawn crept between the curtains of his room. For a moment he thought he was a child once more, and the sea was calling to him for an early swim. Then he remembered what he had seen last night and he struggled from beneath his covers, wiping the sleep from his eyes as he pulled on a dressing gown and went down stairs.

The fire had died in the grate, a pile of grey ash, a few embers still glowing at its heart. Toby was lying sprawled over the chair, his head thrown back, his mouth half open, snoring gently. An empty whisky glass was on the floor by his limp hand, and one of Max's mother's old books was open on his lap.

The girl hadn't moved.

Max ran a hand through his tangled hair, sticky with salt spray from their escapade the night before. He glanced once more at Toby, then headed into the kitchen.

He had just put the kettle on to boil and was rummaging in the cupboards for tea when a creak of the floorboards behind him signalled that Toby was now awake. He turned to see his friend yawning and stretching in the doorway.

"Care for a brew?" he said.

Toby nodded. "Your mother has some interesting books."

Max grinned as he reached for two mugs, the kettle starting to whistle. "Yes. Local history was a bit of a hobby of hers. What were you reading?"

"Couple of things. Firstly, did you know that this isn't the first time there's been a spate of unexplained drownings in this town?"

"No I didn't." He handed Toby a mug of tea, steam coiling up into the cool air.

"Yes. It seems that about two hundred years ago nearly twenty souls were lost. Some of them simply walked into the sea and drowned. Just like the girl was trying to do last night. There's a memorial to them in the churchyard."

"I know it," said Max, leading the way out from the kitchen, back towards the living room. "But I always thought they were from a ship."

"And something else. I think I know what's causing the marks on the girl's arms. I think it's a kind of worm, a parasite. I want to take a closer…"

But Max had stopped. He felt Toby stumble into him from behind and heard the slap of spilt tea landing on the tiles. He was staring at the empty sofa, the blanket crumpled on the floor.

"She's gone!" he gasped. Then something cold clutched at his heart. The mug slipped from his clasp and shattered on the floor. He felt the hot tea scalding his slippered feet and heard the sound of broken pottery skittering over the tiles. And then he was running, flinging the front door open wide. He stared up and down the street but there was no sign of her. Yet he knew where she would be.

"The sea!" he gasped as he started to run. He could hear Toby close behind him as he pounded over the cobbles, his breath forming pale clouds in the frosty air. He could feel the early morning chill through his pyjamas as his dressing gown flapped open, and he lost one of his slippers on the salt drenched steps that led onto the sea wall.

Here he stopped, staring at the sea. The tide was in, grey cold waves punching at the base of the wall, stirring the seaweed and flotsam and other washed up debris into eddies. But the girl was not to be seen.

Max knew in his heart where she was. The sea had called her home, just as he could hear it calling to him now. He remembered the joy of the early morning swims he had taken in the summer as a boy. It was winter now, dark storm laden skies and a steel grey sea, but he could remember the euphoria of the salt water against his skin. And he wanted to feel that way again.

"I think I know what causes it," said Toby beside him, labouring for breath. "You said that she recommended the wrasse to you?"

Max didn't answer. Further along the beach he could see the breakers surging and curling as they dumped onto the sand, and the sound of their roar filled every sinew in his body until it felt that his very being was singing in unison with the surf. Away from the land the swell heaved and rolled like some vast animal starting to wake, and he felt a strange envy of the seabirds that skimmed its cold surface.

"I found a mention of the wrasse – the fish they've been catching of late, in one of your mother's books," said Toby, the sea breeze whipping his words away. "It seems that there was an old folklore that those fish must never be eaten, that they are cursed, but around the time the twenty lives were lost the fisheries failed and some folk started to eat the wrasse instead of throwing them back as had always been the way.

"Now the fish stocks are failing again and once more the wrasse are being served. It's my theory that the fish carry a parasite and that parasite is passed on to whatever eats that fish. But the parasite needs to return to the sea in order to complete its life cycle. And to do that it must compel its host to return to the sea. That's what happened to the girl, to your mother, to all of them…"

But Max wasn't listening any more. He licked his lips, tasting the salt and grit, and a half remembered tang of fish as he walked over the sand. He felt Toby pull on his arm but he wrenched himself free. The waves rushed up over his feet as he started to run, soaking the hem of his dressing gown, but he didn't care. The same way he didn't care about the purple sinuous marks that he could see starting to form on the backs of his outstretched hands. The sea was singing to him and he reached out to embrace it. The sea was calling him home.

HEAVEN SENT

Tagg strolled beneath an indigo sky pricked with stars. The night was wonderfully clear and crisply cold, threatening a frost, yet Tagg walked barefoot between the campfires. The grass underfoot was moist and the earth between the grasses was dusty and dry and he relished the sensation.

Tagg could see campfires scattered across a wide fertile plain, with patches of cultivated ground between clusters of semi-permanent tents. People were gathered around these fires, eating, talking, listening. Tagg now turned moving quietly, the way lit by flaming brands pushed into the earth beside these tents, towards where a group of people were sitting on logs around a fire. Their attention was concentrated on an old man with a long grey beard who was telling them a story about the First Age of Man, his voice low and melodic. Tagg stood at the edge of the firelight, half in, half out of the shadows, listening, large amber eyes fixed on the flickering flames, and long fingers flexing to the rhythm of the words.

The people sitting around the fire were a mixture of men, women and children of a range of ages. They were all grubby and unkempt, for these people lived out their lives tending their crops by day, and in the shelter of these makeshift tents by night. In the evenings they gathered around their fires and listened to the elders speaking of the days long past.

One of the women seemed to sense Tagg's presence and turned, peering into the darkness. Her face was in shadow and the firelight lit her auburn hair from behind with a rusty glow. She recognized Tagg and smiled, then shifted herself along the log to make more room and patted the space beside her. Tagg decided to accept her invitation and stepped out from the shadows to join her. The old man paused briefly in his tale, a look of mild annoyance in his eyes, then continued, waving his arms around to add emphasis to his words.

The warmth of the fire added to the old man's words. Tagg was entranced, despite having heard it many times, for it was an old story. It was told around the campfires most nights, each orator embellishing it slightly, but the fundamental elements still remained; the First Age of Man, when there were only two kinds of people, and only one moon in the sky.

As the storyteller started to speak of the moon Tagg noticed that the sky had assumed a silvery glow behind the shadows of the far mountain range, and now the first moon was slowly emerging from below the jagged horizon; a silver orb of such great beauty. Tagg never ceased to admire this moon for it was constantly in a state of flux, rising and setting at different times, sometimes full and round and at other times just a thin sliver of light.

The old man was talking about these phases of the moon. He was relating the legend that it had not always been this way. He said that during the First Age of Man the first moon had been as constant and unchanging as the second moon now was. But then the second moon appeared in the sky and stole the position that the first moon had held. The first moon has been roving ever since, trying to decide where best to sit, hiding her face in shame from the second moon, then looking to see if it was still there, and on seeing that it still was, hiding her face once more. The old man told the story well and the audience was captivated.

The woman, May, touched Tagg's hand.

"Care for a beer?"

"Please."

She whispered something to one of the children, who eyed Tagg suspiciously before scurrying off into the darkness, soon to return and nervously present a pewter tankard of warm foaming beer. Tagg thanked the boy graciously but the lad just gave a wary scowl and fled. Tagg sipped the beer, enjoying the taste and the sense of euphoria that the alcohol brought. Beer was a peculiarity of these people, but a tradition he was happy to embrace. May turned and smiled again.

May was the nearest thing that Tagg had found to a friend amongst these people. Most were suspicious at best and hostile at worst, but May was warm and gentle. And she was clever. The old legends, told in the firelight, had never truly satisfied her curiosity. Tagg thought how wise she was to feel that way.

They had met in a thunderstorm, while Tagg was hurrying home along the dusty track that led past the campsites to the domes. May was sheltering beneath an oak tree, watching the lightning dance across the evening sky and the misty shroud of rain approaching from the distant hills.

Tagg had spotted the danger she was in and, leaving the track, ran through the long grass towards her, grabbing her arm and pulling her away, just before a shaft of blue lightning severed the tree in two. They stood, staring at the blackened wood and smouldering grass as the first large raindrops plopped into the dust. A few warning drops and then the torrent came, quenching the few flickering flames that licked at the still boiling sap of the wounded tree.

"Thank you," she said, looking up at Tagg as the rain flattened her hair. "I'm May."

"Tagg."

May glanced around. "Come," she said, taking Tagg by the hand. Tagg surprised at this unexpected familiarity, followed her through the downpour towards one of the nearer campsites, its dying fire smouldering on the drenched ground, the people sheltering in one of the tents. They eyed Tagg suspiciously.

It was the first time that Tagg had been in such close proximity to these people; the first time standing amongst them as an equal, in their tents. They seemed mildly suspicious, but not hostile. It was unusual for Tagg's people to leave the shelter of their domes, unheard of for anyone to stand amongst them in this way. They didn't speak but their eyes never left him.

When the storm at last abated and the fires were relit, May had asked Tagg to join them in the firelight and listen to their tales, and one of the children fetched beer in pewter tankards.

From that day on it became Tagg's way to stroll amongst the campfires, drink their beer and listen to their stories. But always it was May's company he sought. And always she was waiting, patiently, eagerly, the trust building in her eyes.

Tagg's people didn't approve of this newfound friendship. They watched with hollow eyes, in silence as Tagg left the domes in the gathering dusk. Sometimes Tagg was aware of someone watching, listening in the darkness, just beyond the edge of the campsite lights. He knew that they frowned upon this penchant for the company of men and women, disapproved of the way he walked among their campfires at night and listened to their myths and legends.

But Tagg felt a growing fondness for these people, and loved the way they embellished and exaggerated their stories, and cared nothing for what the others thought. But in particular it was May who stirred emotions and affections that were new and strange.

One night they sat side-by-side watching the flicker of the fire and listening to the crackle of the flames, as the beer mellowed their souls, and they listened to the old man telling the story of the moons, and then another tale of the great machines that had once helped with the ploughing and the harvest. Afterwards as the other folk retired May and Tagg sat together by the dying embers staring up at the sky, the stars and the moons. And May had turned to Tagg.

"This is all nonsense isn't it? This stuff he was telling us about the moons," she said, her eyes clear as though she had learned a great truth. With a tongue loosened by the imbibed beer Tagg had answered honestly, looking deep into those eyes that seemed to see so much more than her fellows.

"Mostly. The first moon has always been like this. It's always waxed and waned. If you lived by the sea you would see that it controls the ebb and flow of the tides."

"Oh, I've heard of the sea. Is it a long way from here?"

"Yes, a long way. It would take many weeks to get there."

"So people couldn't have travelled there in a day?"

"During the First Age of Man, yes. They had machines then; machines in the air and on the sea."

"And were there really only two kinds of people?" May urged Tagg to continue.

"Yes, men and women. That was all."

"Oh."

The First Age of Man had been so long ago. All these people knew was the Second Age of Man. Tagg looked away from her, to the campfire, the flames flickering in the breeze, uncomfortable, for such matters were never discussed outside the domes. He placed his beer on the bare earth. It had loosened his tongue and answering her in this way suddenly frightened him. She moved beside him. He looked into her eyes again, and now Tagg didn't care what the others might think. Why should these people live their lives shrouded in ignorance, believing the old myths and legends, sheltered from the truth? It had been their world once.

"So tell me about the Second Age of Man?" May persisted taking hold of Tagg's hand. Tagg flinched at her touch, her hand soft and warm, the skin smooth, the clasp tender, and felt the emotions stirring within him surge with a new and unfamiliar passion.

"Yes, the Second Age of Man," Tagg murmured. "The Second Age of Man is now. There are two moons in the sky and three kinds of people. Men, women and neuts."

"So how did the neuts come to be here? If they weren't before," she pressed.

"The neuts came with the second moon. It brought them – brought us here." Tagg smiled gently at May and she smiled back at *it*. For Tagg was an *it*, neither man nor woman. Tagg was a neut.

"And the machines?"

"It's better that the neuts control the machines. It's a better world this way."

"And the Third Age of Man?"

"Then all will be in harmony."

At this May had fallen silent, and Tagg stared at her, finding her suddenly beautiful, even though she was not of his kind. And Tagg had pondered what the world must have truly been like, back in the First Age of Man. He remembered how their old world had died, how they had come to this new world, and how much had changed since they arrived.

The old man paused in his rendition of the tale of the two moons and glared hard at Tagg, for May was whispering in his ear. He could feel the tickle of her warm breath and his heart was racing. The old man's dislike of Tagg was reflected by the glares of the others, for although May welcomed Tagg as a friend, the attitude of the rest of these people hadn't warmed or changed over the weeks.

May whispered again, "Let's walk," and Tagg nodded. They rose in silence and began to move away from the firelight into the shadows now cast by the moon. Behind the old man continued his tale, and Tagg could sense a lightening of the people's spirits as they watched him leave.

As they walked Tagg noticed that the second moon was beginning to rise. This moon was smaller than the first moon, and always rose and set at the same time. Although it shone its light was dimmer. Only the first moon's light was strong enough to cast shadows. They were soon some distance from the fire, walking alongside a field of corn, not yet ripe, dark and rustling in the moonlight. Ahead of them the second moon was partly obscured by the branches of a small copse of trees.

They arrived at the copse and Tagg, still holding May's hand, led her over to a fallen log and urged her to sit.

"Tell me about Harmony," May said suddenly, gazing up at Tagg intently, her eyes bright, dark pools in the moonlight. Tagg was surprised. She hadn't pursued this line of questioning since that night they had sat together by the dying embers. Tagg knew her look was one of admiration and love, knew she felt honoured to be singled out like this, to be Tagg's chosen companion, and smiled at her warmly.

"Harmony comes with the Third Age of Man, and the Third Age of Man is coming soon," Tagg explained. "We live upon the third planet in this system. Have you seen the other two? They appear as stars near sunrise and sunset."

"Oh yes, yes I've seen them."

"Well, in the Third Age of Man all will be in harmony. The third planet with three kinds of people will be lit by three moons."

"And when will the third moon come?" May was almost whispering now. Tagg smiled. May was sharp and quick. She deserved an honest answer, and Tagg had something to show her.

"Come." Tagg stood up and led May out from the shadow of the trees. The campfires formed isolated pools of golden light strewn across the moonlit plain. The mountains rose in rugged silhouette beyond. Tagg pointed to the sky, just beyond the mountains. "Look."

Just above the shadowy peak of the highest of these distant mountains, a small glowing disk had appeared in the sky. May was staring at it in amazement. Tagg suppressed an urge to laugh. Sometimes these people seemed so foolish.

"What is it?" May asked. Tagg could see that she was trembling.

"Do you not know?"

"The...the...third moon?" She turned to Tagg, eyes wide with surprise.

"Yes. The third moon approaches. Soon it will join the other two in the sky. It will be smaller than the first moon but much larger than the second. When it has joined them then the Third Age of Man will begin."

"And all will be in harmony?"

"Yes, three moons around the third planet where three kinds of people live in harmony."

"How do you know these things?" She was staring at the sky again. Tagg felt obliged to answer her, although he wondered whether even she could possibly comprehend the enormity of it all.

"Because the second and third moons belong to the neuts. The second moon was smaller and faster. It brought the advance party here many centuries ago. Our job was to get things ready for the colonists who come in the third moon. Our world was dying. We needed to relocate. So we were sent ahead to…" Tagg faltered for he almost said 'to conquer'. He paused, looking down at May. Her people didn't know, they didn't remember. They had only their legends of a mythical First Age of Man. "The third moon was slower. It took longer to get here." he said softly.

"Oh." As Tagg had feared, it was clear that she didn't really grasp the implications. She turned and suddenly gave Tagg a kiss, gentle and fleeting but a kiss nonetheless. Tagg stepped back in surprise. Something turned over in his stomach. He had taken their friendship too far. The others were right. He should not have become so involved with these people. Still, with the coming of the Third Age, the coming of the colonists, he would no longer have time for such frivolities. There was much to be done.

May was staring up at the sky again.

"The third planet," she murmured. "With three moons and three kinds of people, in harmony."

Tagg looked at her, suddenly sad. His heart was thumping and strange emotions twisted round inside him. He didn't want to give her up. He reached out and touched her, turning her towards him, wondering how much longer he could make this last. Even though he knew that the others were right; that in the Third Age of Man there could be no future with a slave.

THE ARCTIC TRIANGLE

The bridge was in semi-darkness. Rob sat in the Captain's chair, watching the raindrops trickling down the windows and listening to the dull throb of the engines, which he felt through the deck and the seat rather than heard. He could smell the acrid stench of the echosounder readout scorching its trace onto the chart paper, and the stale smoke on the breath of the crewman who was standing nearby, peering out of the window into the gloom of the half-night, his binoculars hanging from a strap around his neck.

Rob stifled a yawn; the dog watch, when everyone else on the ship was sleeping. He hated this shift but as second Mate he took what he was given, and it made him more determined to get his Master's ticket soon. The engines clanked and the rain lashed the windows as the ship rolled gently in the swell.

The crewman stiffened and lifted his binoculars. Rob slid down off the seat to stand beside him.

"See something?" he asked.

"Not sure. Thought I saw a light."

Rob picked up a second pair of binoculars that were hanging from the rail below the window and peered out into the gloom. There was nothing to see. Nothing but an empty ocean, which blurred with a cloud grey sky into a pale haze of drizzle and mist. Nobody, not even birds and whales came here unless they had to.

He put the binoculars down and moved over to study the radar display. The orange line swept slowly round and round as if counting away the seconds of his watch. It was almost hypnotic as it picked up the peaks of the nearby waves in vivid orange, which faded to brown as it passed on its way. There was nothing else out there. But then, why should there be anything else here?

"There it is," said the crewman. "It's moved round to starboard, and come closer."

"There's nothing on the radar." Rob yawned, stretching his arms.

"Well there's definitely something there, and it's coming our way."

Rob picked up the binoculars once more and peered out over the wind-lashed sea. It was barely dawn and the rain on the windows blurred his view, but this time he saw it: a single light in the gloom, appearing and disappearing as it rose and fell with the swell. At times it was hidden by thin drifts of sea mist and the rain that came in short squally bursts, yet always it was drawing nearer. There was still nothing on the radar.

"Any ideas?" he asked. The crewman shrugged his shoulders.

"It's not a ship," he said, and a moment later added: "It's going to pass across our stern."

"Idiot!" Rob grimaced, watching the light bobbing up and down. "Can't they tell from our lights that we're towing?"

The crewman shrugged again and Rob drew in a deep breath between clenched teeth. Maybe it was nothing to worry about. Perhaps it was just a buoy that had broken free from its moorings and was drifting with the wind. But if it was it had come a long way. This part of the Arctic Ocean, although now ice-free, was usually deserted, the shipping routes keeping to the Northwest Passage, hugging the coast. They hadn't seen another vessel for nearly a week, and weren't likely to either. Why did things like this always have to happen on his watch?

"We have to stay on this survey track for the next half hour," he said, speaking aloud to himself as much as to the man beside him. "So we'll keep on this course and maybe it'll just drift past, whatever it is. I'll make a note in the log."

He lowered the binoculars and was about to put them down when he felt his skin prickle and a shiver of electricity passed up his spine. Suddenly the air seemed to be full of tiny sparks of light as if a multitude of minute fireworks were going off all at once. And the last thing he heard was his own voice screaming.

"Sir, we're picking up another transmission."

Sergei moved over to stand behind the man who had just spoken, a thin man with deep sunken eyes whose head seemed swamped by his headphones.

"That foreign frigate?"

"Well there's no-one else here."

Sergei nodded. They had been following that frigate for five days now, across the emptiness of the ocean, an ocean that had once been solid ice with nothing but seals and polar bears moving on the surface. The ice and the bears had gone, but this was still a place where few men came.

"It's being jammed again," said the young man and Sergei scowled.

"Can you tell where it's coming from?"

"Not exactly, but it's nearer this time. Hold on – they've just fired a missile!"

"Damn it," Sergei snarled, clenching his hands into fists by his side. "Whatever are they firing at?"

Nobody answered. Sergei scowled at the lights flashing on the radio equipment that lined the wall, and the deck rolled slowly beneath his feet, a movement that now he barely noticed. What was that frigate following? What could possibly have drawn it across the Arctic Ocean in the middle of winter, when there was nothing but darkness and endless rain, and the eerie banks of fog that formed where the once frozen waters met the warmer currents encroaching from the south? This was an ocean in crisis; a symptom of a changing world.

The young operator removed his headphones and leaned back in his seat, glancing up at Sergei with his hollow eyes.

"Nothing. It's all gone quiet."

"What about the other frequencies?"

"Nothing. The transmissions just stopped."

"What about the sonar? We must still be able to pick her up on the sonar?"

A second operator who had been sitting quietly in the corner of the room now looked round and shook his head.

"No. All her engines have stopped too. She must be dead in the water. Either that or she's vanished."

"Well that's a bit odd," said Sergei running his fingers through his bristly hair. The frigate couldn't know they were following her. To all intents and purposes they looked like any other Russian deep sea trawler, although maybe with a few more aerials than usual. There was nothing to indicate their true role – a Russian spy ship.

They had taken all the usual precautions; staying just beyond their quarry's radar range, no transmissions that might be construed as anything other than a fishing vessel, and a merchantman's flag. No there was no way that frigate could suspect anything. So why had she suddenly gone quiet?

"There was that Canadian Seismic survey ship that disappeared up here last year," said the sonar operator, his thick accent betraying his Black Sea roots.

"I've heard that," said the radio operator. "They're likening this place to the Bermuda Triangle."

"Oh really," snapped Sergei. He turned and left the room.

On the bridge the First Mate was drinking strong coffee and staring out into the night. Sergei joined him.

"Everything all right?" he asked, and Sergei nodded.

"Seems we've lost our frigate though."

"Oh?" the Mate put down his mug. "Well she's out of range of our radar. Would you like me to move closer?"

"Might as well."

The ship now underway they stood in silence staring out at the sea. The rain had abated and a full moon appeared and disappeared between the shifting clouds, lighting the whitecaps and the spray thrown up by the bow of their ship as she pitched into the swell. The ocean between was oily and black and beyond in the darkness was nothing; an empty ocean at the end of the world. Sergei glanced once more at the radar, but the screen was blank, just the nearer wave crests, no sign of a ship.

As he looked back out over the sea he thought he saw something moving towards them through the darkness. He squinted his eyes and peered into the gloom. There seemed to be a light approaching, but it was a light beneath the surface of the water, like a small patch of moonlight that was still there when the moon was hidden by cloud and darkness enveloped them once more.

Suddenly it seemed that the air surrounding him was crackling with static, and lights popped and vanished, dazzling him. The last thing he heard was his own voice…

# #

The Captain stepped back from the radar display and stared out over the empty ocean, its surface rippling in the moonlight like the crude oil beneath its seabed that was the cause of all the conflict. The civilian was standing by his shoulder, eyes wide, magnified by his spectacles.

"Any sign of it?"

The Captain drew a sharp breath between his teeth. Scientists! Too many questions and no answers. He frowned.

"Only that Russian spy ship that's been following us for the last three days. We could spark off a diplomatic incident if we stray any closer to their waters. Did you know he's jamming our transmissions?" His jaw tensed as he spoke. "It would really help if I knew what we were looking for," He gave the civilian a stern glare. This man was one of those boffins who didn't know his place and acted as if he was in charge. But it was the Captain who was in charge, and he deserved an explanation.

The scientist didn't answer; he merely removed his glasses and started to wipe them on his shirt.

"My cabin, now," said the Captain turning on his heel as the ship pitched into the swell. "We need to talk."

The scientist followed him from the bridge into his cabin without a word and sat watching as he poured them both a brandy.

"So Joe," said the Captain handing him his glass. "Are you going to tell me what's going on?" He unbuttoned his collar and sat down opposite, watching as Joe's long fingers stroked the outside of his glass before finally raising it to his lips.

"I suppose," Joe said. "We've come this far. I've kept you in the dark long enough."

The Captain didn't reply. He sipped his brandy and waited. Joe continued: "We're looking for an Auto-Miner," he said, glancing up.

"An Auto-Miner? Is that all?"

Joe studied the brandy in his glass. There was something furtive about the look in his eyes, as if he was very uncomfortable talking about this. But an Auto-Miner? Why would they come up here looking for one of those?

"There's more," said Joe, clasping and unclasping his fingers around the bowl of his glass. "What do you know about the Auto-Miner programme?"

"Just what I've read – An experimental automatic mining sub – for gathering minerals from the ocean floor and other such inhospitable places. Send it out, and a few months later it comes back to unload its cargo."

"That's right, but there was just one problem."

"Yes, the failure rate was too high, they were always breaking down." The Captain laughed. "Bit like our fleet. They're always cutting corners and doing things on the cheap. So I take it the programme wasn't scrapped after all?"

"No." Joe seemed to come to a decision and downed the brandy in one mouthful. He put the glass down and his eyes seemed to have hardened.

"So what's so important about this one then? Other than the fact that it has no right to be here," the Captain said.

"Have you ever heard of the Micro-Pulse Weapon?"

It was the Captain's turn to drain his glass and he leaned forwards.

"I know of it; a new weapon that was being developed back during the Cold War. That was a long time ago. What does that have to do with sneak-mining the Arctic Ocean?"

He put down the glass and stared hard at Joe. The man was looking around at the bulkheads, the furniture, the floor. Anywhere except meet his eye.

He was about to ask again but there was a tap on the door and one of the crew was standing there, eyes wide.

"Contact Sir. We can't identify it."

Joe struggled to his feet but the Captain reached the door before him.

"I hope you've been telling me everything," he hissed as they returned to the bridge.

The contact on their sonar was small but closing fast.

"We must destroy it now," Joe hissed.

The Captain turned to look at him, wide eyes and sunken cheeks. He looked more gaunt and haggard than ever.

"Don't you want to recover it?" he asked. "If it really is an Auto-Miner and it's been up here all this time then surely its payload of precious metals and minerals must make it worth recovering?"

Joe didn't blink.

"Destroy it now," he said. "Before it destroys us."

The Captain gave the signal and listened in silence as his crew went to work, range and bearing to target, weapons readied and launched, and they watched as the missile was fired and acquired its target. A dull explosion signalled the Auto-Miner's destruction, and the Captain let out a long slow breath.

"So when did we start making things that kept working?" one of the crew muttered to his mate.

"Yeah. Makes a change. Just look at this bucket we're in here. A second-hand ship that probably never worked properly in the first place." Their laughter echoed around.

But they had a point.

The Captain glanced at Joe and raised his eyebrows.

"I seem to remember something about the Micro Pulse weapon," he said slowly. "I remember people saying it was indestructible."

"Not quite." Joe looked the other way.

"I remember hearing that it repaired itself," the Captain pressed.

Joe nodded. "Yes, that's right. It was programmed to patrol the oceans and used the oceans' natural resources to repair itself as needed, extracting whatever raw elements it required from the seabed or from the ocean directly. It could clone any of its component parts, repairing itself as it went along. It was meant to last for ever. But they were never deployed. The Cold War ended. We didn't need them."

"But they weren't destroyed, were they?" said the Captain. "They were used as the blueprint for the Auto-Miner, weren't they?"

Joe nodded.

"So what you are telling me is that that thing we have just destroyed was in effect a Micro Pulse weapon. I take it the weapon part wasn't disabled and that was why you insisted that we destroy it so quickly."

"Well it had to retain some defensive capability. After all, our country has no mineral rights in the Arctic. Any mining mission up here has to be strictly covert."

The Captain sighed.

"Because we're effectively stealing from right under the Russians' and Canadians' noses. It would have helped, Joe, if you had told me all this up front, before we even came up here."

Joe frowned. "I'm not even supposed to have told you now," he said.

A shout went up from the sonar operator.

"Sir, another contact."

The Captain sighed. "In this God-forsaken place. What sort of contact?"

"Another one of whatever that thing was we just destroyed."

The Captain glanced round at Joe. All the colour had drained from his face.

"My God," he said. "There was only ever one. It's done more than just repair itself! It's replicated itself!"

The Captain opened his eyes wide.

"Are you telling me it's out of control? So how many of those things are there?"

Joe shook his head and for the first time the Captain saw real fear in his eyes.

"I don't know," he breathed. "I really don't know."

The Captain was about to reply when the air around him started to crackle and sparkle with a myriad of tiny flashes of light…

ICEBOUND

Dr Tom Johansson stumbled onto the bridge, rubbing the sleep from his eyes and blinking at the sunlight streaming in through the salt-caked windows. The ship rolled and he reached out a hand to steady himself. He could hear the Captain barking orders through the ship's intercom as she rolled again, beam on to the driving Atlantic swell.

"What the hell is going on?" he shouted, but nobody seemed to hear.

The Captain was studying the radar screen, hands placed on either side of the console to steady himself as the ship continued its turn and started to pitch into the waves, salt spray smacking against the bridge windows.

"Full speed ahead," he said, his jaw set firm beneath his grizzled beard.

Tom glanced out at the scene ahead. The crew had set the wipers going on the windows and he could see in the distance, falling and rising amidst the swell, the dark shape of another ship: a black shadow against the blue and white of a wind kissed sea, spume streaming from the tops of the whitecaps. She vanished between the rolling hummocks of steel blue water, to rise again, nearer.

He marched up to join the Captain, the pursued ship an orange blob on the radar screen before him.

"What's going on?" he demanded once more.

The Captain turned towards him and Tom could see the fury in his eyes.

"Bastard cut our tackle," he snarled, gesturing with a work-hardened hand towards the fleeing ship. "Thinks she can get away with it!"

Tom felt a cold shudder pass up his spine.

"Were there fish?" he asked in a low voice.

The Captain shrugged and turned back towards the radar and the retreating ship.

"No, of course not."

"Then what's your problem?"

"What's my problem?" exclaimed the Captain, his face flushing red beneath the grey of his beard and his blue eyes narrow. "My problem is people like that who think they can just cruise in here and take our fish, and employ dirty tactics to stop us taking the fish that our rightfully ours! They think they can just help themselves! These are Danish waters you know, and that..." he jabbed a stubby finger towards the bridge window, "that's a Spanish ship!"

"There are no fish!" Tom shouted slamming his fist down hard beside the radar screen. The Captain blinked but didn't flinch.

"I am the Captain of this ship," he said slowly.

"Captain of a trawler with nothing to trawl for. This ship had been chartered by the Norwegian Government and while we are at sea, I am the Norwegian Government!"

The Captain glared back at him. "I've fished these waters my whole life," he muttered.

"As did your father and his father. I've heard it all before," said Tom. Then he took a deep breath. He felt sorry for these fishermen, he really did. A deep-sea trawler in a sterile ocean that once had teemed with life. But now their nets were empty, their livelihood gone, and many of them, like this man, were still struggling to come to terms with what had happened.

"So we've lost our nets. We weren't going to catch anything anyway. But we've still got a lot of research we can do, measurements we can make. We're trying to help you know."

The Captain didn't answer but gave a swift nod to his Mate and Tom felt the throb of the engines ease as the ship slowed. He stared out at the sea and sky. The sun was low on the horizon, a low as it ever reached at this time of year in these latitudes and he wondered what time of night it might be, for when it was permanently daylight it was hard to tell. He scanned the horizon but the Spanish ship was lost from sight, although he could just make out a dark shadow where the sea met the sky. He scowled.

"Is that land?"

The Captain nodded and prodded the chart laid out on the table beside the radar. "Yes. We're just here and that'll be that promontory there."

Tom frowned at the chart.

"But we're miles from the survey area! How long have you been chasing that ship?" The Captain shrugged in response.

"Do you know these waters?" Tom asked.

The Captain gave a half grunt. "If you could call them waters. They used to be ice. You never used to be able to get this close to land. It was fast ice all the way, and the land was white. They call it Greenland and it really is green now."

Tom ignored his tirade. "Can you take us in closer?"

"I guess so."

"Good." He nodded and stifled a yawn, running his fingers over the coarse stubble on his chin. He felt tired, but there was no point in going back to his bunk. "Then we'll deploy the plankton nets and make some measurements here before we return to where we're supposed to be." He directed a pointed stare at the Captain who paid him no heed. Tom sighed. "Let's see what's going on at the bottom of the food chain." He added and turned to leave the bridge.

Tom stood up and stretched, feeling his joints unlocking and his sinews clicking back into place. One of his research students, a young girl with flame red hair and face a mass of freckles was peering through a microscope on the lab bench beside him, and a tall lanky lad was preparing the next plankton net for deployment. He felt the decks shifting beneath his feet, but the ship was moving a lot less now that they were in the lee of the headland. He turned towards the girl.

"Anything?" he asked.

She didn't pull her face away from the eyepieces but the gentle shake of her head told him "No."

He frowned. Surely the oceans couldn't be that dead? There had to be plankton! After all, the problems with the fisheries were caused in the main by human activity; over fishing depleting the stocks below a critical threshold for recovery when the fish populations were already under stress, trying to adapt to keep pace with the changing ocean circulation. But the plankton? There had to be plankton!

He turned towards Daniel, thinking that maybe he ought to take a closer look at those nets. Maybe they had the wrong mesh size, maybe they were torn, but a flurry of footsteps signalled the arrival of the third of his students, another girl, with yellow hair like buttered straw. Her face was flushed and her eyes dancing.

"Tom, you'd better come up to the bridge and take a look!" she said.

Gelda, the girl with the freckles, pulled her face away from the microscope and the lad, Daniel, paused, net in hand.

"Come on then," he said.

Freyja, the blonde girl, led the way up to the bridge, her boots clattering on the metal stairs. Tom could hear the other two research students close behind him. The coast was nearer now, high cliffs of black basalt. The Captain was scanning the coastline through a pair of binoculars, which he lowered and offered to Tom as he joined him.

"What do you make of that?" he said.

Tom studied the cliffs, at first seeing nothing but barren rock, but then, where the cliffs dropped down to sea level and the water was marked by the muddy stain of a river outfall, he noticed the huts.

"A settlement?" he said and the Captain nodded.

"Looks like it. Nothing on the chart though. This was once a glacier."

Tom could see the telltale ridges of moraine, piles of debris left by the retreating ice. The huts were huddled against the hillside above but he guessed there may have been more, swept away by the scouring of the ice.

"Can you take us in closer?" he asked.

"Don't see why not," said the Captain. "You going ashore?"

"Yes."

"Then I'm coming with you," said the Captain.

"But I thought the Captain was supposed to stay with his..." the blonde girl started to say but Tom silenced her with a glance. He looked at the huts again. They had to be very old. They had to predate the glacier – a glacier that had come and gone. And he wondered what people could have lived here...

# #

They drove the RIB onto the steeply shelving beach of black volcanic shingle and pulled her clear of the lapping waves, the Captain making her fast. Tom stared around at the landscape before him. It was hard to imagine that only a decade ago this whole area had been icebound. But the ice was retreating at an unprecedented rate, the ice sheets that had once covered the great landmasses of Greenland and Antarctica now almost gone, their last remnants being discharged into the oceans in a muddy torrent, like the turbulent orange tinged waters of the river that now flowed where this glacier had once crept.

He stared up at the huts and frowned. He was nearer now, and they looked familiar in shape. Freyja had brought the video camera and she panned round the landscape slowly as they climbed the slope to walk among the ruins. Tom could see how little actually remained of them, just the walls, a jumble of piled stones. In some he could see where a hearth must have once been, and in others he could clearly see the entrance, an outer wall curving round to provide extra protection against the wind.

The Captain scowled and scratched his beard.

"Nobody's lived here for a long time," he grunted. Tom smiled, inhaling the unfamiliar smell of a foreign land.

"A very long time," he said. "If I'm not mistaken this is an early Viking settlement.

The Captain stopped scratching and scowled at him from beneath heavy brows.

"Vikings? In Greenland?"

"Definitely Vikings," said Gelda, brushing a strand of red hair away from her face. She pointed to a large slab of rock jutting out from the ground beside her. "Look what I've found."

Tom joined her and ran his hand over the lichen-coated surface of the stone. It was heavily eroded but the pattern of lines and symbols was still discernible.

"Runes," he said. "I wonder what they say."

"I can read them, I think," said Gelda, looping the rebellious strand of hair back behind her ear. Tom glanced swiftly up at her.

"But what are Vikings doing here?" said the Captain.

Tom smiled. "The first Vikings came here with Erik the Red," he said. "It was during the last warm period, around 900 AD, when Greenland really was green. It was good fertile land and they farmed it for hundreds of years. Then the climate changed and the ice encroached. The Vikings perished. It's a classic example of what happens when people fail to adapt to their changing environment."

The Captain ignored Tom's dig at him.

"Doesn't look very fertile to me," he grunted, looking round at the barren landscape.

"Give it time," said Tom. "This part of Greenland will soon be green as well."

"And this is one of those settlements?" said the Captain.

Tim nodded and Gelda squatted down on her heels, running her fingers over the ancient writings. "Interesting," she muttered, half to herself.

The tall student, Daniel, scrabbled over the loose stones to stand behind her, sweeping his thick hair back into place with his hand.

"What does it say?" he asked, but Tom could tell that he wasn't really interested in the runes. His eyes were fixed on Gelda.

"I'm not sure. It says something about suffering the same fate as those that came before. It talks about the ones who lived on the red hill."

"An earlier Viking settlement?" Daniel suggested.

"Perhaps." Gelda scrutinised the next set of runes. "I don't know these symbols," she muttered.

Tom stared around at the barren landscape. There was nothing growing here yet, for the soil was poor and the centuries of ice and snow-cover had left it all but sterile. He looked around for the plant life that should be beginning to encroach – patches of small tough green plants, moss and lichen covering the exposed rock – but as yet there was nothing. He assumed there hadn't been enough time yet since the ice here had melted. He found himself wondering just how quickly the ice sheets were now retreating, how long before they would be gone altogether.

And there was something else that bothered him. Something missing, but he couldn't tell what. He frowned and scuffed the toe of his boot in the barren earth. This land had once been fertile, and it should be again. But for now he could see the bare exposed rock, and all its folds and structures, and his heart gave a faint lurch as he noticed that the hill behind the settlement was made of red igneous rock.

"Could that be the red hill?" he said, pointing.

Daniel grinned. "If it is, we can see if I'm right about that earlier Viking settlement. Care for a wager?"

"I don't bet," said Tom. "But we'll take a look anyway."

# #

It was clear from some distance as they approached, that the hill was the site of another settlement. Gelda had lingered by the runes and had to run to catch up with them, and Tom could hear her breathing heavily after the uphill jog. He scowled at the ruins up ahead. There wasn't much left of it but this was no Viking settlement.

"It's a walled city." Daniel gave voice to the thoughts tumbling round in Tom's head. "It doesn't look Viking to me."

"I don't think it is," said Gelda.

"No," said Tom. "It's something else. This could be really significant."

He paused before the city walls. Up close like this he could only guess how high they must have been, now crumbling into dust and crushed by metres of snow and ice. Yet from what was left he could see they had been magnificent, the masonry finished to a high standard, as good as anything he had seen in the ancient world.

And to their left was a gateway, guarded by two mighty statues.

"Wouldn't fancy meeting them on a dark night," said Freyja, zooming in on them with her camera. Tom had to agree with her. The statues were of reptilian monsters, badly weathered, but in places he could still see the pattern of their scales carved into the rock despite the centuries of erosion. Their eyes had once been set with stone but were now just hollows, and stubs of white limestone were all that remained of their teeth. But even without fangs they were monsters to chill the heart. He felt an involuntary shudder pass up his spine as he passed between them and entered the city.

Inside the walls the city had not survived so well. There was little to see of what must once have been houses and temples except mounds of rubble. In places the ruins were almost indistinguishable from the heaps of moraine that the glacier had left as it retreated and over which they had clambered to get here.

"Definitely not Viking," said Daniel glancing across at Tom with a grin. "Guess it's lucky for me you're not a betting man."

Tom didn't answer him. He stared around at the remains of the city, wondering who had built it, trying to imagine what it must once have looked like. But there was little enough left to give him any clues. All he could do was guess and imagine.

"There's not much to see here," said Gelda, stopping beside him. "It's not Viking, but that's all I can say."

"And it's not Inuit," said Freyja. "They don't build cities."

"Maybe it's the ancestors of the Inuit. Maybe they once built cities, back when they first arrived here," suggested Daniel.

Gelda shrugged. "Interesting idea. But there would be other cities."

"Unless they were all buried under ice." Freyja said.

Tom kicked a stone and watched it skittering across the bare earth to rebound off one of the rubble walls. He laughed.

"We'll take some pictures and head back to the ship," he said. "Log this find and report back. They can send out a proper team of archaeologists to take a look. Our job is to study the oceans."

"Good," said the Captain, his voice gruff, as he wiped the sweat from his forehead with a grimy handkerchief and started back down the hillside towards the black beach where their boat was waiting. "See one ruined city and you've seen them all!"

Tom saw Daniel look at Gelda and shrug. But for some reason she didn't laugh. She looked quite serious as she turned to follow.

Then there was a shout of alarm that made Tom shiver. He could hear rocks falling somewhere up ahead. The cries grew fainter, as if they were coming from under the ground. And he realised that something had happened to the Captain. He couldn't see him anymore; just hear his muffled cries. He started to run.

The students arrived at the scene before him. He pushed his way between them, peering down, trying to see what had happened. He breathed a sigh of relief when he saw the man below him, scrambling to his feet, rubbing the back of his head with his hand and cursing loudly, his voice echoing amongst the rocks. He had clearly lost his footing on the surface of the glacial moraine and had slipped down its flank as if it was scree, leaving a scar of freshly slipped stone and earth behind him like the track of a grey dusty avalanche.

But then he noticed something else, and Gelda must have noticed it at about the same time for he heard her mutter: "More ruins," in a soft voice beside him.

"But better preserved," said Daniel.

The Captain had stopped swearing and was staring up at them.

"You going to stand there gawping all day?" he growled.

"No," said Tom. "We're coming down."

He set off down the uneven slope, loose rock sliding beneath his feet. The others followed behind him. Occasional stones rolled down past, gathering speed and bouncing off others, causing them to start to slide as well.

The Captain was looking around at the ruins when he they joined him. Tom followed his gaze. The scree they had scrambled down was part of one of the larger moraine deposits left behind by the retreating glacier, but the area they were standing in had escaped the souring of the ice. He studied the morphology of the landscape. It would need a more detailed survey to confirm for sure, but his initial assessment was that the ice had been steered away from this location by a sill of hard igneous rock. And it was into this rock that an entrance had been carved, guarded by the same two reptilian monsters that guarded the city walls on the hill above.

Gelda was kneeling down, looking at the masonry that marked the remains of the foundations of ancient buildings that had one stood in this place. She glanced up at Tom.

"Some sort of temple, I think," she said. "These dragon things are incredible."

Unlike the carvings on the city gate, these were perfectly preserved, white limestone teeth and eyes inlaid with black obsidian. Their scales almost seemed to glisten. Beyond the entrance he could see nothing but darkness, a stream of murky orange melt-water flowing out from between the statues.

"Are you getting all this, Freyja?" Tom asked. Freyja nodded as she panned around the scene with the camera, pausing to zoom in on the carvings, a strand of blonde hair drifting across her eyes.

"Let's take a look inside." He pulled a torch from his pocket and led the way to the temple entrance. The stream of melt-water backed up against his boots, leaving behind an orange residue when he lifted his feet. The cave stank of damp and decay.

Tom paused, looking around the cavern. The others dispersed, Freyja panning with her camera, Gelda studying the carvings and writings on the walls, which were like no script that Tom had ever seen. He caught her eye and she shrugged in response.

"There are some more of your runes here, Gelda," said Daniel. He was squatting in the muddy orange water, running his fingers over the base of a broken stone pedestal. Gelda hurried over to join him, splashing through the water, the floor of the cave flooded, a giant puddle, flowing out through the cave entrance.

Tom joined them and Gelda looked up at him, her eyes wide, fingers tracing the patterns of the runes.

"'*Death came from the skies*,'" she translated.

"It's some sort of altar, I think," said Daniel straightening up. "Only it's been damaged." Gelda continued studying the runes.

"The ravages of time?" Freyja suggested. The camera whirred as she adjusted the zoom.

"No," said Daniel. "This has been broken on purpose. Desecrated. Look!"

The top part of the pedestal had fallen backwards, and Tom could see the scars of the tools that had been used to fracture the rock. He could also see something else; attached to the top of the pedestal but now half submerged in the swirling opaque waters was a lump of rock, its surface glinting metallically in the light of his torch. He moved round to take a closer look. The water was deeper here and he stumbled slightly as he felt it start to trickle in over the top of his boots. It was bitterly cold and numbed his toes. He stooped down and touched the rock, gazing with wonder at the intricate patterns the metal made on its surface. His fingers tingled at the contact.

"It's a meteorite," he said.

"*Death came from the skies*," Daniel quoted. "Do you think it wiped out this civilisation?"

"I doubt it." Tom straightened up, feeling suddenly light-headed. The enormity of what they had found was overwhelming. The excitement was making him shake. "They built this temple to the thing, though. I guess it probably killed a lot of people, but it didn't wipe them out."

"It must have left a massive crater," said Daniel. "They'll probably be able to find it now the ice has retreated."

"Yes," said Tom reaching out with a hand to steady himself, his head spinning.

"Are you all right?" asked Daniel.

"I just need some air."

He felt Daniel take his arm. The melt-water splashed his legs and the cold was biting. Then he was out in the brilliant sunlight once more and he could feel its warmth. He blinked to clear his vision. The Captain was sitting on a rock looking at him.

"You don't look too good," he said.

Tom shook his head. He could sense the students hovering around him and feel their concern. This was silly. He tried to pull himself together but when he tried to stand he nearly fell. He leaned back against a slab of rock.

"We'd better get you back to the ship," said the Captain.

He felt Daniel take his arm and pull him to his feet. Gelda was walking beside him. He gulped in drunken lungfuls of air and his head seemed to clear.

"What did the other runes say?" he asked.

"Don't worry about it," she said, glancing at him, and her eyes were dark.

"No, tell me. It'll make me feel better."

"They said '*Death came from the skies.*' I guess that was your meteorite. The Vikings clearly thought it was responsible for what happened to them and assumed it was the same thing that had happened to the people who built the city. That's why they defaced the altar. Of course, it didn't save them. Nothing could stop the ice."

Tom grinned.

"Fascinating," he said.

"But there's one thing bothering me, though." Tom glanced round at her, the movement making him dizzy.

"What?"

"It's just that this settlement is very old. One of the first, yet it was abandoned early on. Other settlements in Greenland persisted for hundreds of years. This one was abandoned before the ice came."

They had reached the RIB and Daniel lowered him onto the shingle. He looked around. The Captain and Gelda were preparing to launch and Freyja was still filming. Daniel sat down heavily beside him, and Tom suddenly noticed beads of sweat breaking out on his forehead, his dark hair damp. He was shaking.

An icy chill shivered up Tom's spine. This was so very wrong! He looked out towards the others. Freyja was filming the river, its outfall of swirling orange melt-water dissipating into the ocean. And he realised what it was that was missing, what had been bothering him ever since the set foot on shore. There were no seabirds, yet the skies and the cliffs should be full of them. He looked back out at the ocean.

"It's water borne!" he gasped.

"What is?" said Daniel, looking at him, a deep intensity in his eyes. "What are you saying?"

Tom felt his vision starting to blur, and then the black shingle of the beach was rushing up to meet him. He clasped with his fingers against the grit and sand. It all made sense now, the barren landscape, the sterile ocean, two ancient races, their buildings crumbling to dust, the desecrated temple, and now this. It had been sealed in a temple, trapped beneath the ice, but now the ice had melted and water would carry it, whatever it was, to wherever the ocean currents took it.

"*Death came from the skies*," he gasped.

THE SCREECHERS

I took refuge from the storm that night – a decision I would come to regret – but at the time the glowing lights of The Ship Inn were a welcome relief from the driving rain and the dull repetitive swish of my wiper blades. Night had come early with the storm and I was driving roads I did not know, peering through a rain smeared windscreen, trying to anticipate the bend of the road ahead.

And then the lights, swimming out of the gloom, summoning me with the promise of hot food and cold beer. I turned off the road.

The car park was emptier than I had expected and I was able to park close. Even so the storm managed to drench me in the short sprint through the pelting downpour. I jumped one puddle and landed in another with a splash. After that I didn't bother and I ran through the pooling water, shaking the water from my hair as I entered the pub – as if I were a dog.

A barmaid with plump cheeks and thin brown hair welcomed me with a smile. I stamped my feet to shake off the excess water, feeling my socks squelch between my toes. Those puddles had been deeper than I'd thought.

"Bit of a nasty night out there." I shed my coat and leaned against the bar. The pumps in front of me were all labelled with the names of local ales, and behind the barmaid a menu was scrawled on a board in coloured chalk. I pointed to the nearest pump.

"I'll try a pint of this, and pie and chips?"

The barmaid turned to fetch a glass. I leaned back against the bar and looked around. It was your typical English country pub; wooden beams hung with horse brasses and a fire burning in the grate. At the far end of the bar a thin grey grizzled man sipped his beer and gave a nod of welcome. Over by the fire a cackle of middle-aged women gossiped over their dinner, their laughter shallow. Apart from that the pub was empty.

"Quiet night, tonight," I said to the barmaid. "Storm keeping everyone at home?"

As if in answer a blast of wind rattled the windows, seeming to start at one end of the pub and work its way along. The front door slammed open and an icy wind curled round my wet ankles. I darted forwards to push it shut. It was my fault it had blown open – I mustn't have shut it properly when I came in.

But as my hand touched onto the brass handle a new sound ripped through the wind and rain, a sound I had never heard before and have not since, and I hope that I never will again. It was a strange screeching sound, like many voices screaming in agony, shouting to the wind in pain. It was a sound that turned my blood to ice and made my scalp prickle.

It was a sound that didn't belong on this Earth.

I froze, staring out into the blackness of the night. All I could see outside the door was where the light from inside the pub caught the rain as it fell, looking like the shafts of golden arrows. But the screeching kept coming, enveloping me, filling my heart with cold dread.

"It's the wind," said a voice behind me and I turned to see the barmaid. "It does this sometimes when the storms blow in from the west."

"That is no wind," I said.

The barmaid shrugged. "There's a cleft in the cliff above the bay. The wind whistles up it. That's what makes the noise."

"It sounds like people," I said, full knowing how crazy I sounded. I laughed at my foolishness. "It sounds like the voices of the dead."

She reached past me for the door handle, intending to push it shut. But as she did the sky filled with light, a white glaring light that was for a moment like day, then faded to a single brilliant source that drifted slowly downwards, blurred by the mists of rain.

"That's a flare," I said. My voice was half drowned by the screams from the rock cleft; screams that were meant to be wind but sounded so strange and alive that it was hard to accept they were not of human origin.

"A flare!" I shouted raising my voice above the din. The barmaid turned away and returned to the bar, picking up a tea towel, wiping and stacking glasses as if everything was normal.

I followed, leaning over the bar towards her. Outside the screaming did not cease, but at least the sound was muffled by windows and doors. "We should call the coastguard," I said.

She did not answer – her back towards me, glass after shining glass replaced on the shelf.

"It could be a ship in trouble. We should call."

"It is a ship," said the old man at the end of the bar fixing me with me with bloodshot eyes. "And we should not."

"Why not?"

"Because we cannot help them now."

He lifted his pint glass, draining the last of his beer. The barmaid took it and started to refill it. Neither looked in my direction and I shook my head in utter disbelief. She was pulling his pint as if nothing had happened, and this was any normal evening in their local pub. Even the women by the fire were acting as if there was nothing untoward. But it wasn't normal. Those screams were not the wind and now I was certain they were the voices of people, perishing on a foundering ship. I turned for the door and took up my coat.

"Don't go there."

Her voice was firm, commanding. I hesitated for a second and looked round at her.

"Don't go out there. It's not our place to see what we cannot change. You are a visitor to these parts. You do not know."

I didn't answer her. I turned to face the storm.

Outside in the rain the screams were all around me; a deathly screeching that tore through my soul and filled me with dread. I was not a man to imagine things, or believe in ghosts or a higher being. But I did believe what I saw with my own eyes and heard with my own ears – and that flare was real!

The rain battered my face and plastered my hair flat against my scalp. My jeans were already soaked, clinging to my legs. Water trickled down my neck as I hurried across the car park. I pulled out my phone to call the coastguard but the signal was dead, no network, no way of calling for help other than back in the pub I had just left.

Ahead of me the flare still hung above the cliffs. I used my phone as a torch instead and crossed the road as the rain tore down in shrouds. A sloping grassy swathe led towards the cliff top and the screeching of wind or devils swept round me. If it wasn't for the light from my phone I might have gone over the cliff edge as it appeared abruptly before me. I teetered a moment then stepped back to safely. Was it my imagination or did that wailing take on a note of dismay before crowding in on me? The wind picked up pace, buffeting me where I stood, soaked through to the skin. I was one with the storm. So wet now that the rain could not touch me. I looked down at the waves crashing onto the rocks below, fuming and spitting and dashing spray high onto the cliff face.

And there, in the lights from the sinking flare, was the cleft; a jagged black chasm in the face of the cliff. As I watched the noise increased pitch until it grated like the screech of chalk on a blackboard. I lifted my hands to cover my ears.

So it was just the wind after all!

Perhaps those people back at the pub had been toying with me. Perhaps they had their reasons to act the way they did. But there was a ship and the flare was real – a cry for help – yet I was the only one who came.

The ship was a pleasure yacht, tall-masted, deep-keeled. The sort of yacht you would see in full sail hugging the coast, transporting her owners between seaside towns from harbour-side café to harbour-side bar. But that night she lay broken, mast shattered, askew. Her decks were awash with seething foam, lashed with salt spray, her hull crushed upon the rocks.

But that was not all I saw in the dying light of the falling flare, for the sea was more than an angry foaming mass of spray streaked waves and churning foam. The sea was moving in a different way – as if it were a living beast. As I watched I saw that the sea was more than just alive. There were creatures in it, moving with the waters, as if they were part of the waves.

They had eyes and they had claws. In them I saw such savagery that fear hit me, choking the breath from my chest. This was real and not simply some hideous dream.

There were monsters in the seas. I saw that now. I watched as they clawed their way over the decks and into the holds. That was when the screaming started again. Only this time the screams didn't come from the cleft. This time the screams were human – real – and they came from the yacht that the waves were tearing apart.

The last light from the flare died and in those few seconds before the world was plunged into blackness I saw what those monsters were dragging from the hold. I heard the terror in that woman's screams as the sea creatures tore her life from her and the yacht finally splintered and vanished beneath the waves.

But even though I couldn't see her any more I could still hear.

Her screams hung in the air all around me, splintering and coalescing into a cacophony of sound. Then her screams joined the screeching in the rock cleft and they became as one.

At last I understood what the people in the pub had meant when they said not to come. For indeed, against such devilry there was nothing I could do, and to tell of what I had seen would only brand me as a fool.

I backed away from the cliff top, guided by the light of my torch and the glow of the pub. But I wasn't going back in. I turned towards my car instead, trying to blot out the screeechers and their terrible cry.

As the wiper blades started their steady sweep and I pulled back onto the road the screeching stopped.

I pressed my foot down hard against the accelerator and tried to breathe.

I will never come back this way. And I will never again travel by sea. For I know what the screechers are; the screams of those claimed by the monsters that swirl in our ocean deeps and steal the voices of the dead.

SYMBIONTS

Martin charged up the stairs two at a time, his jaw tensed, teeth gritted together and hands clenched into fists by his side. His anger surged like a tide in full flood and his trainers thumped on the marble steps, repeating as dull echoes beneath the high ceiling of the faculty building. Eyes turned towards him and knew that his rage was plain for them to see, but he didn't care. How dare Professor Kermeen!

Sylvie was coming down the stairs and she flattened herself against the wall as he barged past. For a moment he had the impression of brown eyes, wide with surprise, white lab coat flapping open, a short skirt and shapely legs. But he could see the door to the Professor's office on the landing up ahead, and the door was ajar. He would speak to Sylvie later.

He thrust open the door and stopped short, just over the threshold, his breath catching in his throat, his chest heaving. Professor Kermeen was standing by the window and turned in surprise at the sound of Martin's entrance. His white hair was dishevelled and a grey cardigan hung limply over his crumpled shirt. But he wasn't alone. Martin narrowed his eyes and frowned. He recognized the man before him; a tall man with greased back hair and an expensive suit – one of the sponsors who had been at yesterday's presentation, the one who had asked the questions that had made Martin's flesh start to crawl.

The man turned towards him, recognition in his dark eyes, but no expression on his face. Martin hesitated. His rage was unabated but he didn't want to take the Professor to task in front of this man. Not the head of Italian National Security.

"Ah Martin." Professor Kermeen smiled as he spoke but Martin could hear the tension in his voice. "This is a surprise, we were just discussing your research."

Martin scowled at him but didn't reply.

"You remember Alessandro Moretto, don't you?" the Professor continued. Martin could feel the man's eyes probing but didn't turn to meet them. How could he not remember? Those outrageous suggestions he had made! He continued to glare at Professor Kermeen.

"I'm so pleased you've joined us." Moretto's voice was liquid and Martin felt a shudder pass up his spine. "I was hoping we could resume our conversation."

Martin's stomach started to squirm, tying itself in knots, and he suddenly knew what this was all about. He took a deep breath and turned to meet those cold brown eyes.

"I take it you're the reason I've been locked out of the network?" he challenged. Moretto smiled, but it wasn't a friendly smile.

"I'm sure you appreciate that this is a matter of national security. We cannot return your access until we're sure we have your full cooperation."

Martin turned towards the Professor and raised his eyebrows. Professor Kermeen shrugged and avoided his gaze.

"The Professor fully appreciates the situation," said Moretto, and his eyes had hardened, like a predator anticipating his prey's next move.

Martin stared back at him. "You really mean to do it, don't you?"

Moretto flashed his teeth in response. "It's the logical application for your research."

"No it's not! It was never designed to be used on normal people, or on more than one person at a time. The resonant frequency has to be targeted. We've only ever tried it on one man…"

"The subject you introduced us to yesterday." Moretto nodded slowly and his smile became more wolf-like. "Yes, I was certainly very impressed. Your research has come on faster than I had ever anticipated."

"But he was criminally insane, a habitual offender, he couldn't control his violent tendencies, he…"

"Indeed. I saw the CCTV footage of the mugging and the robbery too. And I also saw the man he has become, thanks to your little device, the calm gentle man walking in the garden, listening to the birds singing and smelling the roses. I would say that was a pretty conclusive result."

"But that's just one crazy man – you're talking about using it hundreds of people at once." Martin held out his hands, pleading, but

Moretto just licked his lips. Martin paused, the let his hands drop. What sort of people were these?

"You've taken it haven't you?" he said softly, thinking of the empty bench in the lab he had just left, only his locked out computer terminal where yesterday there had been the tangle of wires and transducers that comprised the system. Behind him Professor Kermeen cleared his throat, but didn't speak. Moretto glanced at him, then fixed his eyes on Martin once more.

"So do we have your cooperation?"

Martin tensed his fists. "No."

"I'm sorry to hear that." Moretto shook his head as if he was sad and Martin gritted his teeth at the insincerity of the gesture. "Well if you'll excuse me gentlemen." He stooped and picked up a briefcase, ran a hand over his greased hair, smoothing it down, and left the office without looking back, his shoulders rigid beneath his suit, his shoes clicking against the stone floor.

Martin turned to the Professor who was stroking his beard and looking out of the window. He was staring at the protestors in the street below, and yet his eyes were unfocussed, not really seeing them. Martin had passed them on his way in, blockading the building across the green where they carried out medical tests on rats and monkeys. There was always someone protesting about something.

"So?" he said, but the Professor shuffled his feet and didn't look round. "Why did you let him take it?"

Professor Kermeen sighed. "I'm so sorry Martin, but it was his to take. He funded your research."

"But he's going to use it for crowd control! It wasn't designed for that! Who knows what will happen."

Professor Kermeen shrugged. "I'm sorry Martin."

"And why have you locked me out of the network? My thesis is on the drive. It's nearly finished!"

"I'm afraid you won't be finishing your thesis, Martin."

Martin felt his jaw drop open and he stared at the Professor.

"What?"

The Professor paused a moment, eyes still fixed blankly on the scene below, and when he spoke it was in barely more than a whisper. "I'm sorry, but your position here has been terminated. You will receive a month's pay in lieu of notice, but I'm afraid I'm going to have to ask you to vacate the premises."

Martin stared at him. He opened and shut his mouth and didn't know what to say.

Martin sat in the warmth of the morning sun in a pavement café on the edge of the *piazza*. His head was thumping from the night before, his pulse throbbing in his temples. He lifted his *espresso* to his lips and relished the caffeine rush that promised to quell his hangover. What on earth was he going to do now?

To one side of the *piazza* a few market stalls had been set up and Martin watched the people as they milled about and argued over the prices, arms gesticulating. Beside the fountain a young couple were kissing, passionately entwined, neither seeming to draw breath and Martin felt himself blush as his eyes lingered. A young man sped past on a *Lambretta*, his hair flapping in the wind, helmet looped over his forearm. He beeped his horn as he passed in support of the picket line outside the entrance to the office building next to the café where Martin was sitting. They waved back to him and Martin glanced at the placards propped up against the wall; a pay dispute. There was always something.

He leaned back and closed his eyes, the gentle warmth of the sun massaging his skin. It was that fresh warmth that comes before the heat of the day and he breathed in the scents of the town, coffee and fresh bread, geraniums, dust and dry heat. He listened to the murmur of voices, the occasional passing vehicle and the background of soft splashing from the fountain, and somewhere on the buildings above him a pigeon flapped loudly from one perch to another. He was going to miss this place.

And then something passed between him and the sun, and he felt a cool shadow where the sun had been playing just a moment earlier. He opened his eyes.

"Sylvie?"

She smiled down at him and removed her sunglasses. He couldn't help noticing the curve of her hips and the bulge of her breasts beneath the light cotton dress. Her smile was generous but her eyes were concerned.

"I thought I'd find you here. You didn't go home last night."

Martin gestured for her to join him and she slid into the chair beside him in one liquid movement. Her dark hair tumbled down to her shoulders.

"What happened?" she said.

Martin shrugged. His head started throbbing worse than ever. She reached across and touched his hand. He looked down at the smooth skin and a tingle passed up his arm. "Professor Kermeen won't talk about it," she said. "What did you do?"

Martin looked into her soft eyes and something lurched inside his stomach. She really cared! And she hadn't turned up here by chance. She had come looking for him.

"I didn't do anything," he said, and cringed at how lame he sounded. "Not like that anyway."

"But you must have done something. They don't just march people out like that unless they think you're some sort of security risk or something." She was frowning, fine creases appearing between her eyebrows. He finished the last of his espresso and realized that he was still shaking.

"It's all to do with my research," he said. "It was funded by the Department of National Security. I thought it would only ever be used in very special cases. It seems that they have a rather more sinister application in mind."

Sylvie looked sceptical. "And I take it you didn't agree with them?"

"Exactly. What they want to do with it – well it could be really dangerous!"

"But you don't know."

Martin sighed and gazed out across the *piazza*. The couple by the fountain had stopped kissing and were sitting, hand in hand, staring into one another's eyes.

"No," he said.

"So what are you going to do now?"

Martin shrugged. "I guess I'll just have to go back home. I'll miss this place." He really wanted to say *I'll miss you* but the words faltered on his tongue. He blushed and glanced towards the picket line. They were waving towards a group of people who had gathered on the far side of the *piazza*. The group waved back and the picketers cheered, then they melted into the side streets and were gone. Martin frowned.

"Perhaps you can sort things out, at least finish your doctorate," Sylvie said.

Martin shook his head.

"You ought to at least try. You can't roll over and admit defeat?"

She was right. It probably was worth putting up a fight. If only to spend a bit more time in her company.

Another group of people had appeared at the far side of the *piazza*.

"What's going on over there?" he said with a nod of his head. The people melted away just as the first group had.

Sylvie looked round. "What, them? Just some people going to the demonstration."

Martin felt as if he had been run through by a dagger of ice. He stared at her in horror.

"What demonstration?" he gasped.

"Anti-globalization protest this one, I think." Sylvie shrugged. "There's a big march planned, right through the city centre. I'll be giving it a wide berth." She grinned at him with a flash of white teeth. Like him she was a foreign national here, but he was sure that there would be plenty of people from the University at the protest. Fear for those people crushed his spirits once more, and his pulse thudded behind his eyes.

"When did they take it?" he said softly.

Sylvie frowned. "Night before last, just after you left work. They were hanging around after the presentation. Came into the lab, unhooked it all and took it away." She hesitated a moment. Then in a hushed voice she said: "You showed them the subject didn't you?"

Martin nodded.

"So what's his story? I heard he was a violent criminal and now he's gentle and calm."

"That's about right." Martin paused. He had never really discussed his work with Sylvie. In fact this was the first time they had exchanged more than a few pleasantries. Somewhere, deep down beneath the pain of his hangover and the more pressing concerns surrounding the demonstration, he was enjoying her company. "If you like I'll explain it to you on our way."

"Way where?"

Martin pushed back his chair and rose to his feet. Across the *piazza* more people were passing in a constant but disjointed stream.

"We need to follow them. They'll have set it up on top of a building somewhere above where the crowd is going to gather, where the transducer beam will give the best coverage of the most people." He swallowed and his mouth was dry.

"Why?"

"We have to stop them," Martin said, and started to walk away. Behind him he heard the scrape of Sylvie's chair and the click of her heels on the flagstones as he hurried to catch him up.

"So tell me what it does," she said adjusting her sunglasses and shouldering her bag. Martin didn't slow his pace.

"Have you ever wondered what makes us different from other animals? What it is that sets up apart from the higher primates?" he said.

"I guess we're just more intelligent. I've never really thought about it." Her heels scraped on the cobbles as she hurried along beside him.

Martin smiled.

"Have you ever wondered why, of all the creatures on this planet, we are the only ones that are not in harmony with it?"

"No?"

They reached the far side of the *piazza* and joined the straggle of people heading along the side streets. Some carried banners, most walked in muttering clusters with determined strides.

"We rape and pillage this planet, strip her of all her assets and give nothing back. We are like parasites on this lovely world. Did it ever occur to you that maybe we don't really belong? That something might have happened to us that changed the way our species evolved?"

"I'm not sure." Sylvie's voice sounded uncertain. She had pushed her sunglasses up onto her head and was frowning at him. "What has this got to do with your research?"

"Did you know that not all intelligent life is corporeal?"

"What do you mean?"

Martin smiled at her dubious scowl. "Did you know that there are beings of pure energy?"

"I don't believe you? We'd know if they were." Sylvie slowed her pace slightly, then quickened it once more to keep up with him.

"They're here now. They drifted in, a long time ago."

Sylvie didn't reply. Martin continued.

"Beings of pure energy can drift across time and space. It must be an empty existence for them. But when they chance across a world where corporeal creatures have reached a certain point in their evolution, a certain level of higher intelligence, they can join with them. They can gain substance, become whole."

"This sounds like complete nonsense to me," said Sylvie. "You're making this up."

"There's a certain amount of conjecture on my part, I'll agree. But everything I've seen in my research, all the evidence, points to this being true. What I did to the subject proves it."

"He's a man. Surely he has a name."

Martin smiled.

"He's more a man now that he ever was."

The density of people around them had increased and Martin took hold of Sylvie's hand to keep her close as they wove their way through the crowd.

"I don't understand what you're telling me," she said. Her hand was soft beneath his fingers.

"At some point in human evolution such energy beings chanced upon our planet, and there they found a race of early hominins, at just the right stage of evolution. And so they joined with them. That was the moment that we became wise man, or *Homo sapiens*, and stepped beyond the other species of our world. That was the dawn of humanity."

"Are you trying to say they took us over?" Sylvie laughed, close to his ear, her breath sweet. "This is ridiculous!"

"No at all. They joined and the two species evolved to become as one. It's a symbiosis. We are not one animal, but two, a symbiotic organism. That is what makes us different from everything else on this planet."

Sylvie was staring at him, aghast and on an impulse he stopped and pulled her round to face him. He could feel the crush of the mob pushing past. He looked deep into her brown eyes, and the dark hair tumbling around her pretty, serious face. On an impulse he kissed her. Her lips were soft and her mouth tasted of coffee and sugar. She pulled back.

"You're a crazy man," she said, but she was smiling.

People were pushing past them and bumping him into her, forcing her closer by increments. They were still in a side street, flanked by tall buildings, colourful washing hanging in the still air above, strung between the apartments. Up ahead the street opened out into what he knew must be another *piazza*, and here the crowd spread out and slowed, the murmur of their voices forming the drumming repetition of a distant chant.

"This must be it," Martin said, and pulling Sylvie along behind him they began to weave through the crowd.

Once out in the open *piazza* the crowd was more spread out and it was easier for them to move through it. Martin scanned the tall buildings, searching. It would be here somewhere. To one side he could see a television van with a satellite dish on top, camera crew waiting. They were expecting this to be big. People were still flowing from the side streets and soon the crowd would become too dense for them to move. By then it would be too late.

"There, above the Bank," said Sylvie, tugging at his hand. Martin stared up into the blue sky, dazzled by the brilliance of the sun. It was there, unmistakable, the conical shape of the transmitter. The crowd was still gathering. The rally hadn't started yet. There was still time.

"Come on," he said, dragging Sylvie along beside him. "We have to stop them." He barged people out of his way, ignoring the curses and gestures in his wake.

"But what are we stopping?" said Sylvie, breathless beside him. "What are they trying to do?"

"I noticed the pattern when I was studying the patterns of human brainwaves." Martin spoke rapidly, never taking his eyes off the building up ahead. Figures were moving around the transducer, and he could make out the distinctive uniforms of the Italian *Carabinieri* standing guard. They would make sure they were well out of the way before they activated it. He pushed an elderly lady out of his way and her handbag clouted him on the back of his head as he thrust his way through the deepening crush.

"The more I studied it the more it seemed that there were two interacting patterns. And in a few individuals, those with uncontrolled violent tendencies for instance, one pattern seemed to dominate."

"You mean the two parts of the symbiont?"

"Yes. In most people the human part and the energy being are in balance, but when one dominates, well, you have people like our subject."

"So what did you do to him?"

Martin glanced round at her. "I killed the energy being, the alien part" he said.

Sylvie stopped, her eyes wide, staring at him.

"You did what?"

"It's what my device does. It transmits a frequency modulated acoustic pulse that exactly matches that part of the brain's signal that relates to the energy being. Increase the level to a critical point and the alien dies. It allows the human half to return to dominance. That's what I did to the Subject."

"But if what you're saying is true then he's only half a man."

"Well yes. But he was a dangerous criminal, an exceptional case. They want to use it for crowd control. They're going to turn it on this mob. The thing is, once you kill half of the symbiont there's no going back. It's dead. It's irreversible. And we've no idea what will happen if you kill the energy being part of a normal person. The subject was insane!"

"Then we have to stop them!"

Sylvie pushed forwards, and now she was leading him. He could feel the pressure of her hand clasping his. But the crowd was denser now and their progress was slow. He looked up at the rooftop. He could see the white gun holsters of the *Carabinieri* as they moved back and forth in front of the transmitter. For an instant he thought he recognized the tall figure of Alessandro Moretto, silhouetted against the sky. They were still working on it. There was still time.

The crowd around them was chanting now, their voices blurring together and the roar of their voices assaulted his ears. Sylvie was saying something, her lips moving, her voice drowned. He tried to concentrate on her words.

"How do you know?" she said. Beyond her he saw a half-brick arc through the air, and a second later there was a yelp of pain followed be a roar of rage, rising as a deep rumble like an approaching earthquake.

"Know what?" he shouted over the racket. They had almost come to a complete standstill. He glanced up at the rooftop, but it was empty, only the transmitter, standing stark against the cobalt sky. They had taken shelter from the beam, leaving it on automatic countdown. There was not much time left.

"How do you know it's the energy being you kill, not the other way round?" Sylvie shouted.

Martin paused. The thought hadn't occurred to him, but now Sylvie mentioned it… He had assumed that he was killing off the energy being, leaving behind the human part that truly belonged to this planet. But what if Sylvie was right? What if he was killing the man? And then it dawned on him that maybe it was the animal part that gave mankind his passion and drive. He would be destroying the very essence that makes men human! What was left would be a void, an empty body, and the energy beings would be in control, freed at last from their symbiotic constraints. They would at last truly have become corporeal in their own right. The human bodies would become like the shells on the beach that the hermit crabs use and discard at will.

And then he remembered the news crew he had seen, broadcasting the images of this riot around the world. If the pulse was transmitted they would broadcast that as well. He felt a cold clutch of rising panic.

He shuddered and nearby another brick flew into the air. The crowd roared and surged forwards buffeting them in its wake. He staggered and tried to push his way through. They were so close to the door of the bank, but the press of people was too intense, and he could feel their anger flowing around them like an electric wave.

The hair on the back of his neck prickled and for a moment his vision blurred. He was intensely aware of Sylvie's hand pulling away into the crowd. He clung to it and felt her fingers slipping through his. And then it was gone and he was swept along with the tide of human rage.

"Sylvie!" he shouted, but he couldn't even hear his own voice.

His head throbbed and his vision blurred again, but this time it was slower to clear. He felt a surge of panic and there was a humming sound in his ears. And then the world spun as a wave of dizziness flowed over him with a sudden rush of fear unlike any fear he had ever known. For a moment it was as if he was falling, tumbling, empty and lost, spiralling downwards, the road rushing up to meet him.

His vision cleared and he looked around. He felt empty and bereft, but calm. There had been something, something urgent, but it didn't matter now. The square was quiet, full of people staring around. He caught the eye of a woman and smiled. She had soft brown eyes and dark hair tumbling onto her shoulders. He wasn't sure but he had the feeling that she was somehow familiar, as if he had seen her in a dream a long time ago. She smiled faintly and drifted away with the rest of the people.

Martin stared up at the sky. It was such an intense colour. He had never seen anything so beautiful, and the intensity of it crushed him with an emotion that he couldn't name.

He stood for a long time, staring at it.

DISCORD

Andy stretched, leaning back from his desk. The window was open and the voices of children playing in the street below drifted in with the sunlight. He glanced over at the clock on the wall and sighed. Lucy wouldn't be here for ages.

He rose to his feet, and started to walk back and forth in front of the window. Perhaps he would leave the essay marking for another day. And then his eye came to rest on the sheet music that he had taken from Professor Matravers' office, lying on top of his piano, where he had dumped it all those weeks ago. Lucy had wanted him to have it, even though he had never met her father, even though nobody knew for certain that he was dead.

Andy stopped pacing, picked up the pages and looked at the Professor's writing. He hadn't tried to play it. It would sound dreadful. He could see that plainly. But it was an enigma. The sheet music that these pages had been found with was aimed at a high level of ability, but these handwritten notes looked like a cacophony of noise without a single correct chord. How could anyone who could play so well write so badly? Why would the professor have written such awful stuff down?

Lucy had had no idea when he asked her. Although close to her father she had never shared his interest in music, and the whole thing was a puzzle to her as well. Andy smiled as he thought of her, and felt a light flutter in his stomach. Yet he was curious, remembering what Rory had told him when he arrived in the faculty; how Matravers had been playing his piano just before he disappeared.

And then he began to wonder if it really would sound so bad.

Perhaps he should play it and see?

He sat down in front of his piano. It was plain, brown wood and coffee cup rings, nothing like the fine work of art he had seen in the professor's office. But it played well and that was what mattered most. He ran his fingers up and down the keys a few times, listening as the scales hung in the air, then turned his attention to the music before him.

He started to play, and the sound was just as dreadful as he had expected it to be. A few bars into it he was about to stop and play something sensible, but then he heard something else. There seemed to be another sound coming from beyond the notes, as if the off-key scramble of tones were recombining to form something new and strange. Intrigued Andy continued to play, picking up speed as he did so, for, somehow, the faster he played the more tangible the weird sound became. His breath came in short gasps and a trickle of perspiration ran down the back of his neck. What was this music?

And then the room began to dim.

The sensation was unnerving, as if he was losing touch with his surroundings, and he wanted to stop. But now the music held him, a strange compulsion to play ever faster. His fingers fluttered over the keys, and the other sound seemed to be throbbing within him. And then he saw the first of the shapes; a shifting shadow on the edge of his vision where the room had dimmed the most, something moving, reaching towards him, a human figure, and yet, not human. He struggled to pull his eyes away from the music and looked towards it, and then he saw that it was not alone. There were others, crowding behind, all stocky of build with thick shaggy dark hair and heavy brows, their mouths gaping wide in a soundless cry, white teeth, sharp canines, half man, half beast.

Then he heard them, their guttural voices, speaking a language that he could not understand. But he knew that they were pleading with him. Another voice sounded from the shadows behind them, a scream; a human scream.

Then something was pounding, thumping, and his fingers faltered. As the music slowed the strange apparitions began to recede, and the room around him brightened. The banging sounded once more and this time Andy stopped playing. The room was bright, spring sunshine pouring in through the window and outside a thrush was singing. Someone was knocking on the door.

He looked over at the clock and stumbled to his feet. His shirt was clammy with sweat, sticking to his back as he pulled open the door. Lucy was standing there, smiling at him.

"Hi," she said. "I wondered if you were going to let me in."

Andy grinned sheepishly.

"Sorry. I was playing." He held the door wide to let her past. She was clutching a pile of books which she placed on the table.

"The stuff my father wrote?"

Andy nodded and Lucy rolled her eyes as if to say 'What a frightful din.'

"My father's old journals." She gestured towards the books "I thought they might interest you as you were asking about his work." She took off her glasses and wiped them on her shirt, squinting at him as she did. "You OK?"

Andy forced a smile. He was shaking. What had just happened? What had he seen? He could still feel the intensity of his fear, and tried to dismiss it, yet the whole experience had an eerie quality as if something was just out of reach. He shook his head to try to dispel the feeling. Lucy was here now. He must just have been dreaming.

"Yes, I'm fine. What's in the journals?" He picked up the top one and started leafing through its pages. Lucy laughed, her voice gentle like a brook.

"Mostly the ramblings of a crazy old man."

"You shouldn't say things like that about your father." He gave her a sideways grin and turned back to the pages before him. And then he saw something that made his heart lurch. He flicked back a couple of pages. There, in front of him, was a sketch; a drawing of something half human, savage. A picture of one of the creatures he had just seen.

"Andy?"

Lucy's arms were around him, her soft eyes filled with concern. He dropped the book to the floor. Don't think about it. It isn't real. He kissed her.

"I'm OK. Just a bit tired."

"Not too tired I hope?" She was smiling at him now, her eyes creasing slightly at the corners.

"No, I'm fine," said Andy and kissed her again.

That night Andy lay awake. Lucy was curled up beside him, her arm draped across him, her breath gently stirring a strand of hair that had fallen across her face. But Andy couldn't sleep. He couldn't get the sketch in the Professor's notebook out of his mind; the grimacing face, the haunted eyes. And he thought of the shadowy faces of the creatures he had seen that afternoon.

He pushed the duvet aside and slipped out of bed, pulling on his boxer shorts. Lucy stirred but did not wake. He crept through to the living room, lit with the orange glow of the streetlights outside, and silent but for the loud ticking of the clock and the gentle growl of the engine of a car passing in the street below.

He picked up the pile of journals and took them over to his desk, switching on his desk lamp as he pulled up his chair. He flicked through the topmost volume until he found the page he wanted. The creature snarled out at him, wild hair and desperate eyes, teeth somewhere in between a snarl and a scream. Andy shuddered. He turned his attention to the text, scribbled in the Professor's long sloping hand beside the image and started to read:

> *"Today I saw the banished. It was just a glimpse but*
> *enough to convince me that the shamans are wrong.*
> *This was not meant to be."*

Andy paused, looking at the words before him, but they made no sense. Who were these creatures? Were they the banished? And if so, where? And why? A mumble of voices rose and fell outside the window and somewhere two cats squealed and hissed in the dark. Andy turned back to the pages of the journal, skimming through the earlier entries, then pausing to read in more detail.

> *"Today we set out across the desert. I am excited by*
> *the prospect of what I might find. For years I have*
> *been fascinated by the recurring theme of an*
> *underworld throughout mythology, call it Hades or*
> *Hell or one of its other many names. But perhaps a*
> *parallel world would be a more appropriate name,*
> *and one of many at that. But this one is different. This*
> *one can be reached from ours. I feel as if all my*
> *research is about to come together into something*
> *monumental. Maybe the shamans will provide me with*
> *some answers."*

Andy paused, gnawing on his thumbnail. He read the passage again, then skimmed through the next few pages, for the entries were brief, describing the journey and the professor's observations along the way; unusual rock formations; a ruined city; a stop at an oasis. Then there was a gap of many days before another entry that Andy paused and read with care.

"This last bout of malaria was by far the worst I have suffered to date and has left me feeling weak. I doubt I will survive another attack. I have been sick since arriving here in the village. I could barely cling to my camel's back. But yesterday I was well enough to be invited to join the shamans by their fire. I do not speak their language, and my guide struggles to interpret as much of what they say seems to be beyond his comprehension. But they speak of a race of people who were banished to a place that is here and yet not here. And tomorrow they will open a portal to this place to prove to me the truth of their words. I am trembling with awe and anticipation and can barely sleep. A portal to a parallel world? Can such a thing be really true?"

The following page bore the drawing of the creature that had first caught Andy's eye. He quickly turned it over and began to read the next day's entry, running a shaking hand through his hair as he did.

"I cannot put into words the experience of the ceremony I witnessed last night. What I saw, those creatures, defies description! I could hear their voices, their language strange to my ears, yet I know the shamans understood whatever they were saying, although they gave no reply. I have written down the notes of the strange music the shamans used to open the portal, as best I can remember them. I have not told the shamans. They welcomed me to their fire again this evening and warned me never to tell another soul what I saw last night. As if I would! Who would believe me? They will not tell me the reason for the banishment, but alluded to a great king, in the days of the melting ice. I believe that they were

banished at this one man's decree. And they kept on
repeating that what was done cannot be undone. I
think they know that the banishment was wrong.
Tomorrow I leave their village. And with this
knowledge I will return home a different man!"

The next few pages described the journey home, with no further comment by the Professor on his experiences in the mountains, just the everyday observations he made as he travelled. Andy flicked through them, scanning the words, looking for something that might give him some clue as to what he had seen through the portal, for he knew now that he could open the door that the Professor had written of. He had seen the other side with his own eyes. If he hadn't seen them himself he might well have thought these the scribblings of a crazy man. But what had he seen? And then something caught his eye.

"I have tried to play the music but my old fingers are
not quick enough. I cannot open the door. But I can
just see them, on the other side, looking back at me. I
can see the despair and pleading in their eyes. They
are human, and yet not human. I still do not know who
they really are."

As he read these words a folded sheet of paper slipped from between the pages and fell to the floor, landing by his feet in the darkness beneath the desk. Andy put down the book and stooped to pick it up. He unfolded it, realising as he did so that a cold grey light was filtering in through the windows and outside a bird gave a single shrill call. Others responded and the air began to fill with birdsong. He stared at the page before him. It was a photocopy of an article from an anthropological journal. And there was a picture looking out at him, not snarling, not grimacing, drawn with a quizzical expression on its face, but unmistakably, the same creature. He read the article through twice, then put down the paper and turned to the final journal entry, dated only a few days before the Professor's disappearance.

"I now know the truth for what it is, and I struggle to
set it all down on paper while it is still clear to me. At
the dawn of mankind Homo neanderthalensis lived
alongside Homo sapiens, two species of man, in
balance. But as the ice retreated the shamans of our
ancestors banished them, at the whim of their king, so

that only the one race of people remained. This explains the mystery that has long puzzled the scientific community of what happened to the Neanderthals. No-one could possibly have guessed the truth! So who is worst, the banished or the banisher? Perhaps those other people have a right to return. Perhaps there should not be only the one species of man on the planet. Nature has been forced off course. It is my calling to redress the balance. I can feel it. But fever shakes my hand. I know that I shall not survive another bout of malaria. Yet I know what must be done, and I hope that, should I fail, whoever reads these words will not dismiss them as the delirious ravings of a foolish old man, but will take the music and open the portal. The world we live in was not meant to be. The shamans were wrong in what they did. Their evil must be redressed. The banished must be allowed to return from their exile and the world returned to the balance that was its true destiny. I will try. I will try."

Andy stopped reading and leaned back in his chair, staring at the journal before him. Somewhere in the distance the wail of a police siren sounded and he could hear more cars and the voices of people passing on the road outside. He rubbed at the stubble that was starting to bristle on his chin. Back in his bedroom Lucy was still asleep, and the world was quiet. But what world was this? This was the world the Shamans had created. And somewhere, separate from this dimension, the Neanderthal people suffered in their exile.

Andy was shaking, and his mind felt strangely fogged. The Professor's words had touched him deep inside, and the faces of the banished haunted him. What if the Professor was right? What had really happened to him? They said he had just vanished into thin air. Rory had spoken of it to him, over a beer one night when alcohol loosened his tongue. He had heard the Professor playing his piano late in the evening. And then the music had stopped and the Professor was gone.

Andy knew that it was up to him now. He glanced towards the bedroom door and smiled as he thought of Lucy lying there asleep. She knew nothing of this. He felt suddenly closer to her than he had ever felt to anyone before. And he felt closer now to the Professor. He was the only one who could really understand. He was the only other person to have seen them.

And he remembered the voice he had heard, a man's voice calling, screaming from the shadows, a human voice, begging for help. And he knew whose voice it was he had heard, trapped with the banished on the other side.

He rose to his feet and started to pace the room, running his hands through his hair, the floorboards creaking beneath his footsteps. Then, abruptly he came to a decision. He strode over to the piano and sat down. He held out his hands, flexing his fingers, watching the tendons as they tensed. Yes. He would do it. He had to know. He could help Matravers. He could help the banished.

He stretched out his fingers and began to play. Once more the room around him dimmed and the shadowy figures began to take form, until he could see their eyes shining and hear their strange voices. And then a lone voice, a human voice screaming:

"No! Stop playing! Don't let them through!"

Andy felt something cold clutch at his heart. He tried to stop but it was as if he had no will of his own, as if something else was compelling him to keep playing. The Professor's shouts grew ever more desperate.

It was too late, for the first of the figures was in the room beside him. And still he played on.

WEEDKILLER

SPRING:

Spring came early that year and Tom strolled down the lane to his allotment, listening to the birdsong. Daffodils bowed to him in the spring sunshine and the fresh smell of mown grass drifted from the gardens.

The allotment was a tangle of dead stalks and straggly weeds after the winter frosts and Tom set to work, pulling up the remains of the last year's crops, piling them onto his compost heap and clearing the few weeds that had set root over the fallow winter months.

Old Jack in the next allotment was hard at work too, leaning on his spade to catch his breath, his face flushed red and his smooth scalp reflecting the sunlight.

He nodded towards Tom in welcome. "You missed one."

Tom scowled at the freshly dug earth. "Did I? Where?"

"Over in the corner where your sprouts were."

Tom followed his gaze, blinked, and blinked again. So he had. How on earth had he missed that?

The weed was huge, at least two feet wide. Large furry leaved spread from its crown and overlapped one another like so many tongues, and at the centre a clump of short spiky tendrils thrust their way towards the sun.

Tom picked up his fork and went over for a closer look. Now he could see that the fur on the leaves gave them a silvery hue and the tendrils were tinged with gold. He leaned over it and scowled. Yes, he remembered it now. He had seen it the last time he was here. He had been about to dig it up. But now he came to think about it he couldn't quite remember.

And it was really rather beautiful. Not like a weed at all.

"Fancy a brew?" said Jack propping his spade against the side of his shed. "I'll get Maud to put the kettle on."

Tom glanced up at him. Just for a moment he had forgotten that Jack was there.

"I thought you were going to shift that thing last time," said Jack. "Looks like you'll have a tough job of it now. It's grown a fair whack."

Tom looked back at the plant. Its leaves were shimmering in the sunlight and the soft fur on was inviting his touch. It looked like a plant that wanted to be stroked.

"Well don't just sit there staring at it all afternoon," said Jack with a gruff laugh. "I can give you a hand if you like."

Tom tensed, and said "No," before he could stop himself. The blood rushed in his temples. Nobody must touch his plant.

"Have it your way," grunted Jack with a shrug. "Come round when you're ready." He turned the key in his shed door and started off down the path. Tom watched him go. Then reached out for the leaves.

They were soft like the finest down, and they seemed to quiver at his touch. A deep calm surged from his fingertips through his whole body.

SUMMER:

"It's getting bigger."

Tom looked round. Jack had stopped digging his potatoes and was leaning on his spade mopping the sweat from his bald shining head with a handkerchief. He pointed towards Tom's allotment.

"That weed of yours. Weird looking thing. Waiting to see what it turns into?"

Tom looked round to where Jack was pointing.

Of course. The plant. Odd. He had quite forgotten it was there.

And it had grown. A lot. The furry leaves now spread almost onto the path that ran between his patch and Jack's. Amongst the golden tendrils nestled a large red bud.

"That's going to be some flower," said Jack. "Have you any idea what it is?"

Tom shook his head and moved closer to the plant. He wanted to reach down and stroke its soft leaves but hesitated. Jack was watching. He flexed his fingers behind his back. Why was it of any interest to Jack anyway? It wasn't his plant. It was none of his business.

"Big bugger, that rat."

"What rat?" Tom scowled.

Jack shifted his weight against his spade and for a moment seemed to be about to go back to work.

"The dead one, lying there by the path all last week. You took your time shifting it."

Tom shook his head. He remembered something now that Jack mentioned it. But it was too fuzzy, too distant. Had there really been a dead rat lying there for a whole week?

"Ha," said Jack, "You're having me on." He put down his spade and wandered over to look at the weed. Tom's hands clenched into fists. Jack was close enough. Too close. He was bending down.

"Don't touch it!"

Jack straightened up and took a step back. He was frowning.

"All right Tom. I won't."

Tom took a deep breath. "I mean, yes. I got rid of the rat. It was starting to smell."

Jack nodded and turned back to his potatoes.

Tom looked at the plant. It seemed to sense his presence and the faintest of flutters shook its leaves, a tremor of anticipation and it settled them wider, as if awaiting his touch. Tom obliged. He ran his fingers back and forth, back and forth. His hands tingled.

He was vaguely aware that Jack was watching him, as if through a fog – so distant now. Even the sunshine and the summer heat blurred into the background. There was just him. Him and his plant.

And then the rush was upon him, surging through him.

Nothing else mattered.

#

AUTUMN:

Tom raked the leaves from the path between his and Jack's allotments and looked down at the plant.

It was flowering now, huge red petals that twisted into fantastic shapes like origami. A gust of wind blustered through the trees and the fine fur on the plant's leaves shimmered as they stirred in the breeze.

It was beautiful. The most beautiful thing he had ever grown.

"Looks like Mrs Jenkins is still looking."

Tom glanced across at the sound of Jack's voice. He was sitting in a deck chair in front of his shed, pouring tea from a thermos. He nodded towards the lane.

Mrs Jenkins was pinning a notice to the allotment gate.

"You'd think she's have given up by now," said Jack. "Poor thing probably got run over. That's what usually happens to cats."

Tom nodded. A cat. Yes. He remembered something now. His brain was so fuzzy these days. Nothing seemed very clear.

"Been a few cats gone missing recently mind," said Jack slurping his tea. "Catnappers probably." He chortled to himself, ending with a wheezing cough.

Mrs Jenkins finished posting her notice and moved on down the lane, a roll of posters under her arm. For all the good they'd do. Tom had the feeling that she'd never see that cat again. Such a strong feeling that he almost knew it to be true – as if he had seen that cat somewhere, dead, half shrivelled. He shook his head. No. Too hazy. He must be remembering something else.

"Pretty fine flower that," said Jack nodding towards the plant.

"Yes, pretty fine."

"I guess it was never a weed in the first place," said Jack. "You were stringing me along. So what exactly is it? I've been gardening half my life and never seen anything like it."

Tom shrugged. When he tried to think about it his brain started to fog. Maybe Jack was right. Maybe he had planted it. He just couldn't remember.

"Well I can find out for myself if you won't tell me," said Jack screwing the lid back onto his thermos flask.

"You do that then," said Tom, looking back towards the plant. Jack could do what he liked. Why should he care?

"I suppose you're going to go all weird on me again now," said Jack putting his deck chair away. "You're going to go and start stroking it again aren't you? You know, I think it's all a bit odd. Not natural at all. You and that plant."

Tom ignored him. *Go home Jack*, he thought. *Leave me alone.*

The plant was waiting for him. Opening its leaves. Inviting him in.

And the next thing he knew he was beside it, crouching down to stroke its beautiful foliage. Somewhere in the distance Jack's voice niggled but it was so far away now.

The tingling sensation spread from his fingertips and his whole body shook with pleasure. The flower seemed to get larger the more he looked at it.

WINTER:

There was a seedpod there now, huge and swollen, ready to burst. Tom stared down at it, his breath frosty in the chill air as the sun sank low over the hills. The dying light cast a red glow over the clouds, clouds like the tendrils of his plant.

Tom couldn't remember how long he had been standing here.

The leaves rustled in the icy breeze and the tendrils quivered, reaching out to him. Any moment now that seedpod would burst, scattering seeds into the evening sky with explosive fury. Tom didn't know how he knew this. He just did.

"Tom, get away from that thing!"

He looked round and Jack was hurrying towards him, stumbling over the uneven ground, waving his arms.

Jack, always interfering. Tom gritted his teeth. This was their moment, him and his plant. Why did Jack have to go and spoil it?

"Get away from it!" Jack paused on the far side of his allotment, as if afraid to come any closer.

"What are you talking about? Why should I?"

"Tom, it's dangerous. Trust me."

And now Tom laughed. Why should he trust Jack? They had barely spoken these last few weeks. Jack was just jealous. That's what it was.

"Tom, look around yourself. You spend every day here and yet all your crops have run to seed and your allotment is choking with weeds. You don't speak to anyone. You just sit there and stroke that plant. I tell you, it's dangerous."

"Mind your own business, Jack," snapped Tom, squatting down beside the plant. He reached with a trembling hand towards those velvet leaves, leaves that seemed to open before him.

"Don't," shouted Jack. He took a step forwards, then stopped. "Don't touch that thing!"

Tom ignored him.

"Listen to me Tom, I've been trying to find out what that thing is. I asked a few questions, sent off a few letters, and I've been called – just now, by some Brigadier!"

"A Brigadier?" Tom looked round. Jack was hopping from foot to foot. His forehead glistened with sweat.

"He's sending round a decontamination squad! They'll be here any moment now. He said not to go anywhere near here – that they'd deal with it. But I had to warn you Tom. The Brigadier said that if that seedpod opens ... well they've spent all summer clearing these things from around the country. They thought they'd got them all."

"I've no idea what your problem is," said Tom. Jack's words washed over him, meaningless. The plant was calling to him, sweet scent, touch me, *touch me*. The tendrils reached towards him.

"Please Tom," said Jack. "Just listen to me!"

But Tom wasn't listening anymore. In the distance he could hear the wail of sirens. They were coming, coming to destroy his precious plant. But they were too late. Jack was a fool!

All that mattered was the plant.

He reached out and touched its soft leaves and it quivered with pleasure. The tendrils reached out, stroking his face, caressing. Tom closed his eyes. Somewhere in the distance voices were shouting. The first of the tendrils penetrated his skin.

The last thing he was aware of as the rush consumed him and the pleasure gave way to pain, was the seed pod bursting open and a thousand fine seeds floating up into the sky.

RETURN TO ALLER

A spark that burned like fire jolted up my spine and there was solid stone beneath my boots once more. I sucked in sweet air through tight clenched teeth, air that smelled of autumn leaves and bonfire smoke. I was back. I opened my eyes and the world swam before me in a giddying rush. I clasped my fingers against the pummel of my sword and braced my legs. The world steadied and came into view.

Guthrum stood before me in a beam of multi-coloured light that the sun had cast through the stained glass windows. It lit his hair like a halo with the gold of summer straw and I joined him as he stood, staring at the limestone bowl that was the font. There was water in it, still and clear. I reached out with my forefinger and touched its surface, so cold, so icy. A chill passed up my arm and to my heart as the ripples spread in perfect circles. This was where it all had changed.

"My Lord," I said and my voice croaked in my throat. It had been year; a year to the day.

He looked round at me, eyes icy blue, his beard tumbling russet. He reached out, placed his battle worn hand on my shoulder and smiled.

"Ragnar," he said. "We meet again."

The others had joined us in the sepulchral quiet of that ancient church, twenty nine loyal chieftains gathering close around their king. He looked at us all and unsheathed his sword, held it before him and looked down at its blood-stained blade.

"It is time."

He glanced at the font, where the water was once more still, and his lips parted in a sigh. For this was the font where we had all been baptised, and that was the curse that had trapped us here. I remembered how he had stood before the priests and monks, bound in irons and stripped to the waist, his head hung low in defeat. But now he was proud, he was our king, and we were going to follow him into battle, just as we had twelve hundred years ago.

He turned and strode from the church, and we followed, close on his heels, in a clatter of armour and shields, our soft boots scuffing against the stone. We didn't speak and the autumn air was cold against the back of my throat and dry with wood smoke. Ahead the mist rose in drifting shrouds from the marshes. The crows called from the trees above to welcome us as we passed.

Soon the ground became soft and damp, water squelching out from underneath each footstep and we slowed to a walk. The mist was all round us, turning the hedges and trees grey, but when I looked up I could see the crystal blue of the morning sky. I squared my shoulders and tightened my grip on my shield and sword. It wasn't far now.

Guthrum stopped. He held up one arm to bid our silence and we gathered close around him. I listened to the blood rushing in my head and the sucking of the marshes all around, and then I heard something else. There were people ahead and my fingers clenched onto my weapons at the murmur of voices and clinking of mail. But as I listened it struck me. This was not them.

I peered through the mist and I could just about see them, figures in armour and chain. But they were not Alfred and his men, returning as we did, year upon year, us to fight for our freedom and them to uphold what they had done. No, these were not the men we had come to fight. They bore the same arms and wore the same clothes as we did; more men to fight for Guthrum, and I smiled.

They did not act like men going into battle though, for the bellow of their laughter drifted with the mist as they leaned against their shields and swords and lifted pewter tankards high, clunking them together, then drinking. The smell of warm beer wafted over as the wind picked up and the mist drifted and thickened. I could hear their voices yet I recognised not a single word they spoke. Until one:

"Guthrum."

I stared at my king and there was mild surprise in his clear blue eyes as he met my look. Who were these people?

Then the mist shrouds parted enough to see. On the far side, facing us was the other army, Alfred's army. Yet it was not Alfred who stood at their head, but another man, although he dressed as Alfred had that fateful day. And his army were smiling, as if they already knew that victory would be theirs. My own smile faded and my soul burned with rage. How dare they presume?

Then the man who had spoken Guthrum's name stepped forwards and shouted something to them in his strange tongue and they raised their swords to bang them against their shields and cheered.

Behind them though, Alfred stood, as insubstantial as the mist that drifted around him, and his eyes were cold. For he and his men had been brought back here every year by the curse they had brought upon us all.

But now these others had come to fight alongside us. Perhaps this time the victory would be ours to savour. Perhaps this time we would be set free.

The sword clatter stopped, but the echoes had barely faded when a new sound rose; more cheers and shouts from all round the field and I blinked and looked around, but could see nothing through the mist.

The two armies started to march towards one another through the wet grass. They held their shields ready, their swords brandished high and they shouted as they walked. And the cheers from the people in the mist rose to a roar.

Then Guthrum, raised his sword and yelled his battle cry, and we advanced with the throng towards where Alfred stood. Alfred drew his sword and with his men close beside him, he advanced to meet us. I opened my mouth and roared to the heavens as the fury of war surged through my veins and I started to run, beside my King.

The armies met, theirs and ours, as it had on this day every year for over a millennium. But this time, as my sword struck the shield of one of Alfred's men, things were different. These others had never been here before. It had just been us. But now our battle was their battle and their battle was ours, and the crowds watching were cheering Alfred's men to victory, just as it had always been.

All around me was the roar of battle and the clash of steel and the sweat ran down my face as I dropped my shield and raised my sword.

But the man before me was not the man of Alfred's army I had always fought. This man was different. His skin was clean and perfect, as if the wind and weather had never beaten it, and his hands were soft, his fingers long and smooth, like those of a child clutching the metal sword that he laboured to lift. His eyes were gentle and the fire in them was the joy of a game, not the rage of battle. But before I could stay my hand my blade fell, slicing through sinew and bone and flimsy armour that was not well made; beautiful in its craftsmanship, but not sturdy enough to withstand my sword.

He dropped to his knees, blinking blue eyes and his shield and pike fell from his hands. He reached for his shoulder as the blood jetted in an arc, and stared at his hands, stained wetly crimson as he turned them before him. Then he looked back up at me as the blood fountain weakened to a trickle and the fire in those blue eyes dulled.

I staggered backwards, away from him as he reached out his hands in supplication, then fell forwards onto his face, to lie still. The crows had stopped calling from the trees and the crowd fell into silence, their cheers fading in the fog. The battle continued around me, but they enemy faltered as they noticed their fallen comrade and at the field edge someone screamed.

This was our moment and I pressed forward my advantage. To the side I could see Guthrum surging on with fury, and the men of the living army drew back from his sword.

But Guthrum had no mercy in his soul. And neither did I. We had fought this battle every year for twelve hundred years, our one change of freedom, our one chance to enter the halls of our ancestors. Yet each time Alfred had prevailed. This year was different. This year for the first time in twelve hundred years men of flesh had joined our fray; men who could die, unlike those of us who were already dead. I raised my sword above my head and charged with Guthrum towards the enemy.

But then the wind picked up and whipped the last of the mist away and the owners of those voices finally came into view. There were people, all kinds of people, women and children, men old and young. They stood around the edges of the field wrapped in scarves and thick coats in bright colours, while behind them their colourful horseless carts lined the road.

Then the men of flesh dropped their weapons and both sides, the Vikings and the Saxons, gathered around the body of their fallen comrade, and men in bright green jackets came running forwards from the crowd, behind which blue lights flashed against the morning sun.

But we did not slow. We engaged Alfred with renewed fury and this time, for the first time, he and his men faltered, looking towards the body that lay seeping red blood onto the grass. And as Alfred stared so Guthrum struck and the King of Wessex fell to his knees. This time it was different. The men of flesh had changed it and victory belonged to us.

We had embraced the faith they forced upon us in our defeat, but it was not our own. Each year we came back and fought for the afterlife that should have been ours, and each year they took us back to theirs.

I cheered with all my soul as Alfred fell, and he and his men faded to wraiths in the morning light and vanished like the mist. It was just us standing there as the sky started to spin. And we were free.

I go now at last to Valhalla, to Odin's hall, where I will drink sweet mead and feast on wild boar for all eternity.

REMEMBER NORMANDY

I looked down at my hands, red-stained with blood, tacky between my fingers. The blood was mine. It was in my mouth, a sharp, metallic taste, and my shirt was cold and clammy with it. I touched my chest: broken bone and shattered flesh. And yet I felt no pain.

But I wasn't there, where I should have been. The shouts of the soldiers running up the beach and the crunching rubble of that ruined French town beneath my boots had vanished along with the roar of the German guns. I blinked and my eyelids were heavy with grit, my eyes smarted with tears. I had been somewhere else – a half remembered dream. But now I was home.

I was standing in the churchyard, surrounded by bluebells and I breathed in the sweet scent of honeysuckle. The spring sunshine was warm on my face, and a blackbird was singing at me from the yew tree. I looked up at the church – worn stonework and stained glass. It was how I remembered it. I had always thought we'd marry in that church, and my heart twisted and burned as I remembered Em.

I looked down at the grave before me and froze, for it bore my name, but when I looked again I saw it was my father's grave. Yet the date of his death was so many years on from the day I last remembered. I started to weep for all those years he must have missed me.

I walked away from the grave and round to the front of the church, and there rose a monument that hadn't been here before, a tall stone cross, with lists of names around the base. I read those names, the men of the village, the boys from my school, my comrades in arms as we ran up that beach as the bullets fell like hail, until I came to my own and I couldn't read on.

For I was the only one standing here and I knew not why. I had found peace. But something was wrong. Something had called me back.

I still wept but now it was for all of them.

The vicar passed by, muttering to himself. He did not see me and disappeared into the church. I thought for a moment to follow, but then a rush of memories crowded in on me; running through the fields, scrumping apples from the orchards with my friends, laughing in the summer sun. I wanted once more to see the house where I was born.

In some ways the village was much the same but, as I walked its lanes, I noticed more the things that had changed. The road was lined with cars; strange-looking lozenge-shaped cars in bright colours like flags at a fair, and there were more houses than I remembered, large houses of whitewash and brick. The shop was now a house and the petrol pumps had been replaced with flower borders, but the pub was still there; old men sitting on the benches outside with their dogs at their feet, while from the beer garden came the sound of children playing. I paused a while to watch, wishing there'd been a climbing frame like that when I was a boy.

And then regret came crushing in and I wondered if my own children or grandchildren might have been playing there. Now I was crying for lives that had never been and I left them to their game.

I paused in the lane when I neared the cottage, my parent's cottage, my home, watching from a distance, and it had hardly changed at all. The thatch was newer, the walls painted pink and the trees in the garden had grown. Apart from that, it was as if time hadn't touched it. I swallowed hard and was about to go closer when I heard a footstep on the road behind me, and I turned.

It was Em. Old now, her hair white, her face heavily lined, but her step was lithe and she carried herself with pride. To me all the years didn't matter. She was as beautiful now as she had been the day when I took to my knees before her and offered her that ring.

And she still wore it on her right hand now, for her left hand bore a wedding band. Oh Em, you didn't forget me!

I breathed deep of her perfume as she passed and reached out to touch her hair, and she shivered and turned as if she felt my presence. Then she went up to the cottage and gave a light rap on the door. I stood behind her, soaking up her essence, embracing her with my love.

Heavy bolts scraped back and the door creaked open. A grizzled old man blinked at her in the sunlight.

"Mr Wisniewski?" said Em.

The old man nodded.

"Am I right that you're Polish?" She twisted her wedding ring on her finger as she spoke and the old man watched her with wary eyes.

"Yes?" There was a note of suspicion in his voice, and I scowled as I watched this stranger who had taken over my childhood home... but other memories stirred.

"That's wonderful. I'm Em, from Meadowsweet Cottage. I know you're new to the village and I'm sorry to bother you like this, but it's just that Tom Wilcox has hired some Polish labourers and one of them has had a bit of an accident. None of them can speak any English so we were wondering if you wouldn't mind coming over and translating for us."

She flashed him her broadest smile and my heart melted. How many times had she flashed that smile at me? But his eyes narrowed and he opened the door no further. "It's been many years," he said, "since I spoke Polish. I'm not sure I'll be able to help."

"Oh I'm sure you can help," said Em and she straightened her shoulders. She stopped twisting her ring and opened her hands towards him. "You must remember some? Enough?"

"No," said the old man. "No, I don't think I do."

He shut the door, leaving Em standing staring at the green painted wood. She shook her head and shrugged her shoulders, then turned and retraced her footsteps along the lane. I watched her go, but I didn't follow, although in truth I wanted nothing more. But just to see her was enough. She had her life now yet she hadn't forgotten me. And I was needed here.

Doors cannot stop me, even those fastened with large metal bolts, and I passed through this one and into the cottage. He stood in the kitchen filling a kettle with water, but he wasn't alone. There was a chill in the air that no fire would warm. But he could see none of us.

They huddled together in corners and shadows. Some were naked and many looked starved, sunken eyes and jutting bones, and some were soldiers in uniforms like mine. There had been no peace for these people, the way there had for me, and my heart twisted with pity, for there were women and children amongst them.

The radio on his kitchen windowsill was playing an old tune and he hummed along with it as he spooned tea into a pot. Then he turned and took up a bread knife, to saw slabs from the loaf on the breadboard before him. He paused, mid slice, looking out of the window. He was watching Em as she walked down the lane, and there was something about the way he watched, the way he shifted position, craning his neck to get a better view as she passed between the trees; an unnerving stare that I did not like. She was still my Em, after all these years, and she was happy. Leave her alone. And when he looked round at the boiling kettle I recognised his face. This man was no Pole, and I laughed at the transparency of his lie.

As I laughed he looked round and his eyes locked with mine, and for a moment it seemed he could see me.

His heart was bare now. I could see it all. I could see the cruel twist to his mouth and the blood lust glowing in his eyes as it had when he pulled the trigger of his pistol, pointing its barrel towards my heart. He did not have to shoot me there. I was already injured by the blast of a shell, lying amongst the dust and ruins. But no, to him there was pleasure in killing. War and bloodshed were fun.

I remembered how he had stood over me, wiping the spots of blood from his jackboots with the skirts of another of his victims, a child who lay blood soaked and broken in the rubble nearby. That girl was here, in this cottage with the others, watching. I looked into their hollow eyes, their parchment stretched skin, ribs that jutted against their shivering nakedness, and I saw how great his crimes had been.

I saw him now as he had been then, how he turned and walked away as I had breathed my last, the arrogance in his stride, his uniform that of the German SS.

I started to shake. Now he was here, in this cottage, my home, where I had breathed my first breath and grown. Where I had played with my brothers in front of the fire and laughed at my grandfather's jokes. Where I had loved and been loved and where I had dropped to my knees to propose to Em.

I stepped towards him, clenching my hands into blood-caked fists. I knew in that moment that I would not rest while he remained, and he would find no peace in this place.

He blinked, as if puzzled, then shook his head and looked down and flinched. He lifted his hands and his eyes opened wide and I saw that his fingers were stained with blood that oozed from a jagged slash where the knife had slipped.

He turned to the sink, thrust at the tap with the palm of one hand and the water flowed from the tap, swirling red. I stood and watched him.

No amount of scrubbing would wash those bloodstains away.

Supply Ship

He took hold of her hand as she passed. It was dry and cold, unresponsive to his touch, limp beneath the clasp of his fingers.

"Why don't you join us," he said.

She looked down at him, her grey eyes narrow and icy amid freckles curtained by short red hair, then pulled her hand away.

"No."

He watched, entranced by the curve of her hips beneath her overalls as she walked away between the benches; a sinuous movement that suggested she had adapted better than most to the higher gravity of this world.

"She's out of you league, Mate."

Chip took his eyes off the red head and glanced at the man sitting opposite, round face, lined features and half-grown stubble. He shrugged, turning his attention to the thin slurry on the plate in front of him, which they passed off as food in this miserable place. He stirred it with his spoon, scraping together the congealed lumps that had coagulated on the sides of his plate and looked across the canteen to where Red was taking a seat with some of the other women.

"You haven't got a hope," said Baz.

Chip dragged his eyes away from her and back to his lunch, ignoring Baz who was smirking at him and scratching his stomach, which wobbled beneath his grimy fingers. Chip frowned. How could anyone find enough to eat in this place to get fat? Unless they were stealing rations of course. But he wasn't about to ask. You never asked questions like that.

"Didn't you see the way she looked at me?" he said.

Baz laughed, a deep bellow that vibrated his stomach in rhythm. "Yeah, bit like the way you were looking at that muck on your plate just now."

Chip felt an involuntary grin crack across his face and fought to suppress it. "She'll come round," he said, but Baz shook his head. He nodded towards Chip's plate.

"If you've finished that I'll have the rest."

"Be my guest." He pushed the plate away from him, across the grey plastic surface of the table, stained and defaced with graffiti. "When the supply ship gets here we'll have all the food we can eat. That can't be much longer." He paused, looking over at the women who were huddled together. Their muffled laughter could be heard above the other voices in the crowded room. He hoped he was right. He hoped a supply ship would come here soon. They all hoped that.

He took her hand and pulled her round to face him. Her fingers tensed as she resisted. He grinned at her. She scowled back. As far as the women went on this desolate rock, she wasn't bad. Most were real hard bitches, but Red was different.

"There's just us here now," he said. Baz had gone off shift and they were alone in the makeshift laboratory. She pushed him away.

"Don't even think about it, Mate," she hissed.

His grip loosened enough for her to yank her hand away. She gave him a hard glare and turned back to the transmitter. Chip shrugged. He'd leave it, for now.

They worked a while in silence. He could smell the acrid stench of old solder as she tried to repair the shorted out circuits. This stuff was archaic, cobbled together from whatever junk they had managed to find lying about. But he knew it would work. It had worked for ten whole minutes before shorting out last time. Red reckoned she knew why that had happened and he trusted her judgement. He booted up the computer, watching with satisfaction as the screen flashed into life. Well at least that was his bit fixed.

Red put down her soldering iron and stepped back.

"Sorted. Shall we try her?" She didn't look in his direction when she spoke. He nodded.

"Power her up."

She pressed a switch on the transmitter. A series of lights flickered and glowed and data began scrolling on the screen before him. Chip studied the numbers.

"Looking good."

Red turned towards him and smiled. He felt his stomach lurch as he caught her eye. But then she was turning away from him, turning towards the door, a door that was creaking open. Chip cursed Baz for breaking the moment and scowled as his friend yawned and stretched, his sleep cut short, his ample belly showing white between his trousers and his top as he arched his back and flexed his elbows.

"How's it going?" he asked.

"We're done." Chip could hear the pride in Red's voice as she spoke, and his heart echoed that pride. Baz stopped yawning abruptly and turned to Chip who nodded confirmation.

"But that's great," Baz exclaimed. "You couldn't have timed it better. They've just picked up a supply ship entering the system. It'll be in range of the nav beacon in just a few minutes. Can you get this thing fired up and running by then?"

Chip didn't bother to reply. He turned back to the console, fingers tapping over the keyboard. This time it wouldn't short out and the ship would pick up their signal. This time it wouldn't pass them by, leaving them hungry and desolate, staring into the emptiness of space, an emptiness that echoed the emptiness of the store rooms and the emptiness of their stomachs. This time he knew it would work.

He took hold of her hand, and now she didn't pull it away, she didn't resist. It was warm and soft and it squeezed his gently in return. He felt his skin prickle. Nearly everybody was here on the viewing gallery, but he focussed his senses only on Red, standing beside him, and his eyes he kept fixed on the skies.

It was night and there was a myriad of stars strewn across the blackness. Both the moons were up and one, the smaller, was almost full. He could see its distorted shape and crater-peppered surface. Its orange glow illuminated the barren landscape of their world. He wondered what Red's real name was. But you didn't ask questions like that. Not here.

This was a bleak and desolate world, a frozen desert of a world, so different from home. The stars here shone brighter with a clarity they did not have on the Base World. For here there was no atmosphere to blur them. The Base World would be rising in a few hours, a morning star that preceded the dawn. Back there were the oceans and forests and the cities and farms of his childhood. He didn't like to think about it much. None of them liked to think about home.

And then he spotted it, a dark shadow blotting out the starts, one side of its hull glowing in the orange moonlight, and he felt his heart lift. They had been a year on this rock, isolated, out of contact with the rest of civilisation. But at last they were going to get fresh provisions. At last a supply ship was coming their way. And perhaps they would have a chance to leave.

He could hear a murmur of excitement ripple through the gathered crowd as one by one they spotted the approaching ship, following the signal from the nav beacon, steady and unerring. And Chip knew that even if the thing failed now, even if the transmitter shorted out again or the computer crashed, their luck was about to change, for this ship wouldn't leave or pass them by. And he pulled Red towards him and kissed her.

He felt her resisting as he pressed his tongue against her clenched teeth and held her tight. But then she was pushing him back and she jabbed him hard in the ribs with her elbow, knocking the breath out of him, making him gasp.

"What did you do that for?" Her eyes were narrow and cold.

"I just thought..."

"Well don't think. Leave that to us."

Chip shuddered, feeling crushed by her rejection. He should have known better. He should have left it to her to make the first move.

And then a shout sounded from the front of the viewing gallery and Chip turned and stared into the darkness, at the rocky landscape, the orange glow and double shadows from the reflected light of the two moons. An electric buzz of excitement passed through the crowd, almost audible in its intensity.

The ship was closer now, blotting out the stars, dropping ever lower as it homed in on their beacon. It was moving slowly, serenely, but then in an instant all that changed and Chip gasped in unison with the crowd.

Suddenly the ship juddered and metal tore as the jagged spikes of the rocks she had glided into pierced her belly. The metal of her hull crumpled like paper and flames spewed briefly from the tears, only to be quenched by the emptiness of the vacuum of space. She foundered in silence, explosions from inside ripping her hull, then dissipating as fast as they had formed. She settled slowly onto the rocks and at last was still.

For a moment there was silence, and then the crowd began to cheer.

# #

He reached out for her hand but it wasn't there. She wasn't there. He knew she was here somewhere, but everyone looked the same in pressure suits. He glanced around. Ahead of him lay the ruined spacecraft, and in her holds were the provisions they so desperately needed. But it was the job of others to recover those supplies. His task was to see if this craft could be salvaged.

He walked carefully over the uneven terrain of the planet surface. When he had first been brought here he had found the higher gravity desperately uncomfortable, but in time he had become used to it. Yet in this cumbersome suit on the broken ground he felt as unsteady as he had back then.

He drew nearer to the ship, treading carefully over lumps of scorched and twisted metal and human remains. He fought back the nausea, swallowing bile that burned like acid in the back of his throat. Other figures around him were unloading fresh supplies, piling them onto trucks to take back to the complex. They would eat well tonight.

He paused beside a large hole in the hull and adjusted the torch on his helmet. He would go in here. He would see if he could make this thing fly again. And he felt a wave of optimism wash over him. He could do it. He would get them off this rock. They had built the jammer and the nav beacon from the junk left lying around after the riots and the breakout, after they had been written off and left to die, and had lured the supply ship to them. He smiled as he pushed his way carefully through the jagged metal. And he thought about the Base World, and how much he missed it and longed to see it again.

And he thought about Red, wondering what her real name was and what her crime had been.

HIGH TIDE

Alice Munroe smoothed down her jacket as she stepped out of the ethercraft into the glare of the noonday sun. She paused, looking around, squinting through her visor as the sun beat back at her from the white limestone rocks. The heat was already intense, and the palms of her hands were starting to sweat as she clasped her briefcase.

Ahead of her was a woman, waiting, tanned brown by the relentless sun, her fair hair scraped back from a face that was lined and weather-beaten. She would have been pretty had the harshness of the environment not taken its toll. Behind her Alice could see the farmhouse, perching high on the craggy precipice, painted white like the surrounding rocks.

Alice glanced back at the ethercraft. Its surface shimmered with an iridescent light like a mirage in the heat. The landing pad was halfway up the hill, and behind the craft the land dropped away towards the plain, a haze of green interspersed with a few scattered rocky outcrops, stretching towards the horizon. In the far distance she could just make out the purple shadow of the mountains and above was a sky of vivid blue like cobalt glaze, fired in the ferocious glare of the unrelenting sun.

She drew a deep breath and turned back to the woman. Hopefully this meeting would be a bit more productive than the one at the last farm. She forced a smile but the woman didn't respond. She gritted her teeth. Why did all these people have to be so difficult?

"Mrs Shimmin?" she said. The woman nodded slowly. Alice glanced towards the farmhouse. "Is Jack Shimmin home?"

"He's out checking the fields. He'll be back later." The woman's accent was coarse and it grated Alice's nerves.

"He did know I was coming today?"

"Oh he knew."

"Then he knows how important this is, and that I have lots of other farms to visit."

The woman shrugged and Alice tightened her grip on her case in irritation. These Agrics were just so bloody-minded! But she had to keep calm. If she lost her temper with these people she would never get anywhere. And it really mattered that she produced a result. This was her first assignment. Failure would mean it was her last, too.

"Perhaps I could come in and wait then, Mrs Shimmin," she said as politely as she could. The woman shrugged again.

"If you like." She turned and started to walk towards the house. Alice followed, picking her way along the uneven track, earth cracked and dusty, as the sun beat down on the back of her neck.

Despite its rough and rustic exterior the house inside was well equipped, the way a civilized house should be, spacious and open plan. Air conditioning kept it cool and pleasant and the décor was pristine. Two young children were watching cartoons on a large viewscreen that made up one wall of the main living area, and Alice recognized it as one of those virtual classrooms they used in places like this to allow children who lived hundreds of miles apart to meet and interact. The children looked over towards her and she smiled back.

Mrs Shimmin poured some coffee beans into the grinder.

"I suppose you'd like a coffee," she said. "Take a seat."

"Thanks."

Alice smoothed her jacket and perched on the edge of the chair. The two children huddled together, giggling and glancing across at her. Mrs Shimmin fussed around in the kitchen but didn't speak.

Alice sipped her coffee in silence, mustering her thoughts. The farmer she had visited first that morning had been ignorant and obstructive, although she hadn't helped matters by losing her temper. She couldn't afford to make another mistake like that. She crossed and uncrossed her legs, and sipped the bitter coffee.

Mrs Shimmin started to lay out plates and cutlery.

"He'll be back for lunch," she said without looking up. "I take it you'll be joining us?"

"Thank you. That would be nice," Alice said, putting the empty mug down on the table behind her. Outside she could hear the whirr of an ethercraft. Jack had returned.

He came in, closely followed by two farm hands, boots and overalls already discarded. He was a big burly man with greying hair and a ruddy face, and he smiled warmly at his wife. Then the smile froze on his lips as he noticed Alice. He scowled at her, his brow furrowed. The two young men behind him regarded her with obvious interest.

"You've got a visitor," said Mrs Shimmin, cutting hefty slabs from a loaf of bread.

Jack grunted. "You'd be that agent from the Ministry," he said.

Alice swallowed and pushed herself to her feet, offering her hand. "Alice Munroe."

Jack regarded it but did not take it. Then he turned away and took a seat at the table where the farm hands and children were already settling down. Mrs Shimmin gestured to Alice to join them and proceeded to dish out bowlfuls of steaming broth. Alice sat down cautiously. The two farm hands were leering at her openly. She turned her attention back to Jack.

"So what do you want?" He gnawed on a hunk of bread, which he had just dunked into his food. Alice took a deep breath. He was going to be just as difficult as the last one. She had to stay in control.

"The Ministry has instructed the Agrics to double their corn production," she said. "And I've come to find out why this hasn't happened."

"Have you now?" Jack leaned back and fixed her with a solid stare.

One of the farm hands sniggered and muttered something to his friend, clearly intending Alice to hear, but his accent was too thick for her to decipher his words.

"From the start of last year's growing period, you were told to use the new strain of corn. But last year's harvest was no different to the year before. Not only did you fail to meet your quotas, it looks as if you haven't even tried."

Alice took a deep breath and sat back, her soup as yet untouched. The men looked at one another. And then Jack Shimmin laughed.

"Is that right?" he said, and the two farm hands grinned at Alice, flashing their white teeth.

"I also have to tell you that from this season's harvest anyone not meeting their targets will be heavily fined."

"Do you think you can scare me with threats?" said Jack. Alice clenched her fists beneath the table. This man was no better than the last one. She forced a smile.

"Look. As you must know conflict is now inevitable and we are going to have to step up ore production from the mining colonies on the outer planets of this system."

Jack snorted. "I don't pay much attention to politics," he interrupted. Alice tensed her jaw.

"This is the only planet in this particular system that falls within the 'comfort zone' and as a result is the sole corn supplier for the colonies. If ore production is to increase, so will the populations of those colonies, and so will their demand for food. That is why the Ministry has asked that you, and all the Agrics here, double the amount of corn you supply."

Jack reached for another hunk of bread. "So what?"

"So what? Don't you care what happens?"

Jack shrugged. "Not really."

Alice gritted her teeth "Well, perhaps you could give me an explanation. Why won't the Agrics increase production? Are you even planting the new strain?" She took up her spoon. The soup had gone cold but she forced a smile at Mrs Shimmin and nodded her approval.

"Is that you finished now?" said Jack.

Alice took a deep breath. "No. I'm not prepared to leave without some sort of answer. You are deliberately flouting Ministry instructions."

Jack shrugged and pushed his chair back from the table. He looked as if he was about to leave, to walk out of here leaving her no further forward. There was no point in her going on to the next farm. They would be no different. She had to find the answers here.

"Well you won't mind if I take a look at the fields on my way to the Brew place," she said. Jack froze and glared at her, and there was something in his eyes that told her that she had hit a nerve.

"That's a bad idea," he said.

Alice frowned. She had flown over the fields on her way here in her ethercraft. From above they formed a flat green carpet shrouding the plain, their smooth surface broken only by the jagged outcrops of jutting rock that were the remnant cores of long dead volcanoes.

"It's not safe for you out there alone," Jack added as if he was giving a reason for his comment, but Alice had the feeling he simply didn't want her going there.

The younger of the two farm hands was staring at her.

"I could show you around if you like," he said. "I've finished for the day and it's my afternoon off."

Alice hesitated. She had to admit that she didn't much care for the way the young man was eyeing her up and down.

Jack frowned, then leaned forwards and muttered into the farm hand's ear. The young man nodded and grinned.

"You'll go with him." Jack fixed Alice with a stony glare. "And you'll do exactly what he says." He turned to the young man. "One hour, no more." He kissed Mrs Shimmin lightly on the cheek and left without another word. The elder of the two farmhands followed, giving his friend a playful punch on the shoulder as he went. Mrs Shimmin sighed as she placed a bowl of fruit on the table in front of the children, who were staring at Alice wide eyed.

"Don't mind Jack," she said with a smile.

The young farmhand was still grinning at her. "My name's Darren," he said.

# #

The ethercraft whirred over the plain and Alice stared out at the acres and acres of green fields beneath her. Darren's touch on the controls was gentle and deft and they skimmed lower than Alice had dared to go in her own craft on the way over to the farm, although they were still too high for her to make out any details of the crops below. She glanced at him, taking in the tanned skin and dark hair, the shadow of stubble on his chin and the firm muscles that she could just see hinted at beneath his shirt. He smiled as if he sensed her looking.

"So is it really going to end in war?" he asked.

Alice shrugged. "I wish it wasn't. But there's nothing anyone can do about it anymore."

"I can't imagine any of it," Darren said. "The mining colonies and Alpha City all seem so far away."

Alice sighed. Alpha City was her home. She suddenly missed the bright lights and the high buildings. This plain of fields seemed open and empty, the vastness of the sky intimidating, and she was glad to be enclosed in the ethercraft.

"And as for Earth," said Darren. "I've never even met anyone who's been there."

"Never likely to either, if it's all-out war," she said. She glanced down at the fields below her. They seemed a long way off. Why wasn't Darren taking her any lower?

"So why won't they compromise?" He turned towards her. He let his glance linger and there was something wolf-like in his smile. Alice ground her teeth. How dare he look at her like that? After all, he was only an Agric.

"It's all about economics," she said. "We control the mines and Earth wants the ore. So they won't allow us independence. What's that red light?"

"Oh Blast." A red light was flashing on the console to one side. Darren flicked a few switches. "One of the magnetic couplings has failed. Damn, I'll have to land to fix her." He fidgeted in his seat and Alice sensed his unease.

"Is there a problem?" she asked.

"No, no, it'll be fine." But he didn't meet her eye.

Darren set the ethercraft down in the middle of the green expanse and frowned at Alice. "This won't take long. You stay in here, OK? No wandering off on your own. Promise?" There was an insistence to his voice and Alice nodded. The hatch hissed open and he vanished outside, leaving her, sitting alone, staring out of the window at the emptiness of green and blue. A blast of warm air blew in through the open hatch, yet Alice shivered. She could hear Darren moving around outside and the clatter of tools against the background buzz of insects. Why was he so insistent that she should wait? She wasn't going to stay in here! This was the perfect opportunity to look around. To see what they were hiding from her – to check which strain of corn they were actually growing. She took a deep breath and went outside.

The heat and the ferocity of the sun struck her first and she squinted around from behind her sun visor. When she glanced up at the sky, where the three moons were showing as pale crescents, she felt dizzy. Down here at ground level she could see nothing but green stretching away towards the horizon in every direction. She turned back towards the ethercraft, desperate to look at anything other than this terrible emptiness. Now that its magnetic field had been deactivated, the craft had lost its shimmering incandescent hue and was just a lump of dull grey metal, with Darren clanking and humming beneath it.

Alice breathed in the dry hot air and felt the dustiness of it parching her throat. She started back towards the ethercraft, seeking out its safe, enclosed space, but then she glanced down at the crops around her, and stopped in her tracks. She knelt down and ran her hands over the delicate fronds. She had never seen a plant like this before. This wasn't the standard corn the Agrics were meant to be growing – it wasn't even the original strain.

She looked around. It was all the same. What were these people growing here? No wonder Darren had seemed so loathe to land, or even fly low. And suddenly the reason for the Agrics' hostility became clear. Alien corn – banned since the fungal plague that killed so many! This was what they were hiding.

Her fears forgotten, she marched across to where Darren was lying on his back beneath the ethercraft. He glanced up as she approached, his eyes narrow.

"What's all this stuff?" Alice gestured towards the greenery that surrounded them. Darren frowned at her and sat up, running a hand through his dark hair.

"I told you to stay in the craft."

"Well it's a good job I didn't. What are you growing?"

Darren looked around at the young crops, tender and green.

"What we've always grown."

"But it's not Ministry standard. It's not even the old strain – let alone the strain you were instructed to grow."

"Well of course not. Ministry standard corn won't grow here. This is a native variety."

"Don't be ridiculous! Of course it will grow."

Darren laughed, his head thrown back, white teeth flashing.

"No it won't."

Alice waved her arms in the general direction of the fields and tossed her head to flick back the loose hair that had fallen across her eyes. How could he be so blasé?

"But you know that ever since the fungal blight wiped out half the population of Alpha City only the properly immune genetically modified Ministry approved corn can be grown. You're putting millions of lives at risk!"

Darren gave her a hard stare. "We tried to tell the Ministry why their corn wouldn't grow – but would they listen? They just came back with threats, just like you're doing now. Meet your quotas or else... So we meet our quotas." He glanced at his watch, then gave Alice a sly look. "We have to get going."

Alice felt her flesh seethe and clenched and unclenched her fists. She could feel her temper beginning to boil and fought to keep control.

"What are you talking about? You don't meet your quotas. That's why I'm here! I demand some answers."

Darren didn't reply. He made a few more adjustments to the ethercraft, then rose to his feet and patted the hull as if it was a beast of burden. Alice stood and glared at him. He grinned at her and his eyes narrowed. Then he came over and stood in front of her. He placed one hand on her shoulder.

"We'd better get going."

Alice pushed him away. "Don't touch me."

Darren shrugged and turned back towards the ethercraft. "Well come on," he said.

She paused a moment before joining him.

Darren frowned as he flicked the switches on the console and tapped the light that was still glowing red. An unpleasant grating noise sounded from the engines. He swore softly under his breath.

"I thought you said you'd fixed it?" Alice said. Darren scowled at her as he flicked the transmit switch on the radio.

"Jack, it's Darren. Got a problem, Mate."

Jack's voice cracked into life, distorted with static. He sounded no less gruff.

"What sort of problem?"

"A big one. Can't get this bird off the ground. We're just southeast of Tilting Crag. Should be able to make it there in time."

"Well that's great, that is!" Jack sounded as if he was snarling. "I'm on my way."

Darren flicked off the switch, glanced at his watch and turned to Alice.

"We have to go," he said.

"What do you mean? Go where? I thought Jack said he was on his way."

"There isn't time. Follow me." He led the way to the hatch and it hissed open.

"What? Go out there? Are you mad?"

"We've less than twenty minutes till high tide. We can just make Tilting Crag in time if we leave now."

"What are you talking about? High tide? We're hundreds of miles inland!" Alice could feel the pent up rage knotting the tendons in her neck and clenched her hands into fists, digging her nails into the palms as she struggled against her temper. She just wanted to get back, demand some answers. These were delaying tactics.

Darren gave an exasperated sigh, strode over to where she was sitting and grabbed her wrist, hauling her to her feet.

"Ouch!" she yelped. But he ignored her protests and dragged her out into the glare of the sun and the vast emptiness of the plain. She fumbled to lower her sun visor as she stumbled along beside him, her wrist still clasped in his hand. Ahead she could see the rocky outcrop of one of the ancient volcanic cores rising like a dark blemish against the green velvet smoothness of the plain.

"You think we Agrics are really ignorant, don't you?" Darren gave her a sideways glance. Alice stumbled, the green fronds lashing her legs.

"I never said that."

"You didn't have to. All you people from Alpha City or the mining colonies, you think you're better than us poor farming folk. You think we're a bunch of semi-literate peasants." He gave her a piercing stare. "So do you think you're ready to witness the tidal bore?"

Alice took a deep breath. The crag was closer now but she could still sense Darren's urgency and his pace hadn't faltered. She could feel beads of sweat breaking out on her forehead and her back was damp beneath her shirt.

"Most of this planet is ocean. I know that. And the three moons exert a very strong gravitational pull. But most of the time they work against each other. And even when they do line up," she glanced up at the sky, "like they are now, how can the tides possibly have an effect so far inland?"

Darren laughed but didn't slow.

"Yes, most of this planet is indeed ocean, with just this one super-continent. But you're wrong about the tides. We may be many miles inland but we're not far off sea level."

"Is that why we left the ethercraft?" She could see the rocks looming above her, and noticed for the first time that the lower outcrops were stained red.

Darren tugged her along.

"If we don't hurry you're going to get a closer look at it than you bargained for."

"But it'll destroy your crops!"

Darren tightened his grip on her arm as they started to climb the lower slopes of the crag. Here the soil was not cultivated, just dust and loose stones that slid beneath her shoes.

"It would destroy your Ministry crops. But we're not growing what you told us to grow, are we?" Darren scowled. "Listen!"

Alice paused. Somewhere behind the hum of heat and insects she could hear a deeper roar. She peered out across the green expanse. Now that they were starting to climb above the level of the plain she could see the purple outline of the distant mountains once more, wavering in the heat haze. And then she noticed a dark line in the distance against the green. As she watched it seemed to draw closer.

She gasped.

"It's a tidal wave!"

"It's a tidal bore."

Darren pulled her arm harder and her feet slipped on the loose stones. She fell, breaking his grip. Her pulse was pounding in her ears and her chest felt tight with fear.

"Darren!" she shouted.

"Climb!" he called back. "Climb for all your life is worth!"

She looked up at him as she struggled to her feet, thrusting herself up the steepening slope, using her hands for added propulsion. He wasn't waiting for her! Anger crushed the fear and drove her after him. How dare he? Her foot slipped from under her and she fell once more, feeling the sharp sting as the stones scraped her knees. And then it was on her, roaring in her ears, tugging her legs in its torrid flow, pulling them round while she scrabbled with her hands at the earth and stones, now splashed wet.

The water was in her mouth, salty and bitter and she coughed and almost choked. The ground was slipping away from beneath her desperate fingers. She caught hold of a boulder, rough and abrasive despite its wetness, and for a moment she thought she had found safe anchor. But the tidal flood yanked at her legs and ripped at her skirt and the boulder began to yield, pulling free from the substrate. She felt herself screaming, a watery scream. She could feel it stinging inside her sinuses. Then the boulder was gone.

For a moment she thought she would surely die, and a strange calmness came over her, resignation to her fate. Then something other than the flood was pulling at her, strong hands clasping her shoulders and tugging against the tide. Sand and gravel scraped her knees, stinging the grazes that were already throbbing with the salt.

She opened her eyes. Darren was crouching nearby, soaking wet and breathing heavily. She shivered in spite of the heat. She looked back towards the plain and watched as the wave rushed on, torrid and turbid with suspended sediment, until what had a few moments ago been green fields was now a brown and angry ocean.

"It's an infrequent but predictable event," Darren said. "The first settlers lost their crops to it but soon got wise. We've grown the native corn ever since. It takes two years to mature. So we'll meet you quotas at the next harvest. And as for the blight? This stuff's immune. Oh, we tried to tell the Ministry that too."

Alice didn't reply. She felt too weak to argue any more, too glad simply to be alive.

"You can go back and tell them we'll meet our quotas this coming harvest. You can take the credit if you like."

Alice shivered again but his words echoed and she smiled. Maybe the Agrics weren't so ignorant after all.

The whirr of Jack Shimmin's approaching ethercraft sounded above the rushing water.

ONE IN A MILLION

Matthew dragged his stick along the metal railings, satisfied by the loud rattle it made, and feeling the vibrations in his hand travelling up his arm. He glanced over his shoulder. The three girls were still following him.

It was because he was different. He had always known that he wasn't the same as the other children at school. Most of the time he didn't let it bother him. But recently things had started to change and they wouldn't leave him alone. He pulled a face and quickened his stride. He hated this game.

The girls were whispering among themselves, and one of them giggled. He wouldn't have minded so much if Fiona had been with them, but these three always took things a bit too far. What started out as a game would soon become a torment.

He stopped dragging the stick and let it fall to the ground, leaving it lying on the pavement. Behind he could hear the girls starting to run, laughter on their breath as they came. But he reached the gap in the railings and darted through. He knew they would not follow.

On the other side of the railings was a patch of wasteland, stunted shrubs and wizened grasses. He followed an uneven muddy track that led towards the old forest, the stumps and trunks and branches of the long dead trees stark against the putrid sky. He glanced back once. The girls were pressing their faces against the railings and he could just hear their voices rising and falling with the wind.

"Scaredy-cat, scaredy-cat…" they chanted. He laughed and started to run, relishing his freedom now that he was no longer pursued, splashing through the puddles of yellow slurry that had accumulated wherever the ground dipped. It splattered onto his trousers, but he didn't care. He knew it would rot the fabric and make his mother fume, but they were only trousers.

When he reached the forest he slowed to a walk. The ground here was more uneven, and the path skirted round broken branches and fallen trees, their roots jutting out of the barren soil. In places the rain had eroded the surface soil, forming gullies that cut down into the bare rock beneath. Matthew shivered. The other children said this place was haunted and dared not come. But for him it was a welcome refuge.

The ground began to drop steeply downhill. Here the erosion was more intense, the gullies deeper, and fewer trees still stood. He scrambled over the fallen trunks, feeling the rotten wood crumble beneath his hands and feet. Soon there would be nothing left to show that there had ever been a forest here. And now he could smell the stink of the sea, and see its greyness where it merged with the horizon, in the yellow fug of smoke that was spewing from the chimneys of the factory across the bay.

He scrambled down a steep slope of loose earth and stone, onto the coarse shingle at the top of the beach. To his left a jumble of rocks jutted out into the sea, and there a lone figure sat hunched over a fishing rod. Matthew smiled and set off carefully over the beach, stepping over the empty bottles and patches of oil that marked the tide line. The air was stinging the back of his throat and caught at his breath, and the old man turned towards him at the sound of his cough. He waved and Matthew waved back. Then hastened over to join him, sitting on the tarpaulin sheet that the old man spread to protect him from the dampness of the slime coated boulders. Matthew looked at the waves breaking gently against the rocks and the brown scum trapped in the eddies that formed between the boulders. The fishing line disappeared into the viscous water without a ripple.

The old man smiled and ruffled his hair and Matthew pulled away.

"Oi Gramps!"

Gramps laughed, his voice cracked with age.

"So what brings you here? Those girls pestering you again?"

Matthew pulled a face.

"They keep wanting to play Kiss-Chase." He grimaced. "Yuk!"

The old man laughed again.

"Guess you're just going to have to get used to that sort of thing."

"Gross!" said Matthew, thinking of the three faces jeering at him from behind the railings. He looked at the fishing line, stretching out into the sea, unmoving.

"Would you like to stay out here tonight for a cook-up?" said Gramps. "I've got my stove and some food."

"Cool." Matthew turned back to him. "Have you caught any fish?"

Gramps laughed again and ruffled Matthew's hair.

"I haven't caught a fish in years!" he said, and Matthew could see the tenderness in his eyes as he spoke. Matthew grinned at the old man. He liked being the favourite grandchild. He knew it was because he was different, the only boy. And that made him special.

"Matthew." The old man's voice sounded soft. "You're one in a million."

Matthew glanced over his shoulder and smiled, rubbing his chin as he walked, feeling the soft down that was beginning to grow there. Fiona was still following him. That was good, although she didn't look particularly pleased.

He picked his way carefully over the rotting tree stumps and skirted round the bramble thickets that had started to grow here over the past few years. They were particularly thorny with barbs over a centimetre long, and the scratches tended to fester and took ages to heal.

Fiona didn't know this place as well as he did, and he slowed his pace so that she would not fall too far behind. Ahead he could see the ocean, stained green with an algal bloom, and beyond, the factory, brown smoke pouring upwards before flattening out in the still air.

He rounded the last of the brambles and scrambled down onto the loose shingle and scattered litter of the beach. The rocky headland was still there, and Matthew looked towards it, half hoping, half expecting to see the hunched figure leaning over his fishing rod, waiting for a fish to bite that would never come. But Gramps was gone and Matthew missed him. People just didn't seem to live so long these days.

He heard stones sliding as Fiona picked her way down the bank to join him on the beach. He grinned and turned towards her, but her eyes were narrow and she did not smile.

"You bastard!" she snarled, sweeping her dark hair back from her face.

Matthew stepped towards her, reaching out to touch her, but she pushed his hand away. Her brow furrowed as she glared at him. Matthew laughed.

"Fiona! What's the matter?"

"What's the matter? Do you really need to ask?"

Matthew shrugged. She was being silly. "Yes. I do."

"I saw you…with *her!*" Fiona's voice seemed to catch in her throat and Matthew could see that her eyes were now brimming with tears. He reached out to touch her face again, wiping away a salty drop that was trickling over her cheek. Then he took her hand and pulled her towards him, embracing her gently. She pushed him back.

"You bastard," she said again, wiping the tears away.

Matthew sighed.

"Oh Fiona. You know how silly you sound?"

She didn't reply and he could see that the anger had returned to her eyes.

"You don't own me you know," he said.

Fiona took a deep breath and he could see that she was shaking.

"I know. It's just that when I saw you, with her… kissing…"

"Shh." He stepped forwards, placing his hands on her shoulders. "You know those other girls mean nothing to me. You're the only one I really love."

Fiona nodded. "I do know. It's just I don't like sharing you, with anyone."

Matthew didn't reply. Instead he leaned forwards and kissed her gently. For the smallest fraction of a second she seemed to resist, but then her arms were around him, pulling him close, and he could feel her breasts pressing against his chest. He kissed her as hard and as passionately as he could.

After a few moments they paused for breath and he looked deep into her eyes. She still appeared serious although the tears had gone.

"I wish you were mine and mine alone," she said.

Matthew smiled and gently touched the side of her face. He ran his fingers through her silky hair.

"I know. I don't want to be with anyone else. It's just the way things are."

He turned then, and taking hold of her hand pulled her round to stand beside him, staring out at the sea. The viscous green waves were breaking against the slimy pebbles, which clattered in the swash. The sky was overcast, mustard yellow clouds, the horizon obscured by haze and the brown smoke of the factory, where most of the townspeople worked. He waved his hand in the general direction of the scene before him.

"You know, Gramps had a theory about all this."

"He did?" Her eyes were wide as she looked at him.

"Yes. He reckoned it was the factory... at least, not just the one here, all the others, all over the place. He reckoned that they were what caused it."

"Oh? How could that be?"

Matthew waved his hand at the chimneys. "It's all the stuff coming out; all the chemicals, all the dust. He reckons that's what caused the seas and the forest to die. He reckons that's what made me different from most other people."

"I think your Gramps was a crazy old man who spent all his time fishing in an ocean where nothing lives."

Matthew turned towards her and laughed at her quizzical expression. "Maybe he was," he said and squeezed her hand. "But Gramps was special too."

Fiona didn't reply at first. Matthew felt her sliding her arms around him once more.

"I suppose he was," she said after a while. "Just like you."

Matthew kissed her, tasting the sweetness of her lips, the softness of her mouth, one hand holding her close and the other stroking her long hair. When they paused she held him tightly and rested her head on his shoulder.

"Oh Matthew," she whispered in his ear. "You're one in a million."

Matthew stared out towards the factory, the grey walls and the chimneys. For the first time that he could remember there was no smoke rising, billowing into the festering sky. The factory had closed.

He glanced towards the headland and thought of Gramps, all those years ago, sitting on those rocks, waiting for a fish to bite that would never come. The sea was red now; red with a soup of microplankton and dinoflagellates, and where the waves broke against the rocks they left a dark smear like blood. He took a deep breath and the pebbles crunched beneath his feet as he moved. He glanced back along the shore, and paused. Someone was coming.

The figure was small, hurrying towards him, half walking, half jogging. He recognised her and running a hand through his thinning hair started towards her. The air stung the back of his throat and the pebbles and litter slid in their scum of oil beneath his feet as he hastened along the beach.

He was gasping for breath when he reached her. She held out her hand towards him and he took it in his, feeling how soft her skin was and how small and delicate the clasp of her fingers. And he thought how precious his children were.

"It's time," she said softly, and her eyes were piercing blue, just like Fiona's. Still holding her hand he led her back the way she had come, striding over the pebbles as she scurried along beside him. The old forest was an impenetrable jungle of barbs and thorns, so they would have to go the long way round. He hoped that there would be enough time. He had been with Fiona for the birth of all their children. He didn't want to miss this one.

Lucy was so like her mother, and all the more precious to him for that reason. Fiona had always been his favourite. And of all the children he had fathered, it was the six daughters Fiona had borne him that he loved the most. It was always her house he returned to in the night, whoever he had been with. He always wanted to wake up next to Fiona. If things had been different there would only ever have been her and he would never have bothered with any of the others. But it wasn't his fault he had been born special.

At the end of the beach a flight of stone steps led up to the lane to the village, and there, tucked away between the shop and the cemetery was the cottage. Matthew ran in through the half open door dragging Lucy behind him. His mother was sitting in the lounge with the rest of the children watching a film on the viewscreen and she gestured upstairs with her head when she saw him.

He ran up the stairs two at a time and burst into the bedroom. Fiona was kneeling on the bed, her arms around her sister, and she smiled when she saw him and sat back down. A midwife, grey of hair and skin, was fussing nearby.

"You're just in time," Fiona's sister said, stepping aside for Matthew to take her place beside Fiona. Fiona smiled at him. She was sweating and her grey hair was damp and limp, but her eyes were bright.

"You cut this one fine," she said.

Matthew laughed gently. "I haven't missed one yet."

He kissed her as she sank back against the pillows and took her hand, squeezing it tightly as she screwed up her eyes.

"Just one more push," said the midwife.

And then it was there, the room filled with the cry of a newborn baby, pink skin and white vermix, wet from the birth. The midwife wrapped it in a blanket and handed it to Matthew. There were tears in her eyes.

"It's a boy," she said.

Fiona strained again and a second son was born. She clasped the babies to her chest and looked up at Matthew, eyes shining, and he felt the emotion choking in his throat.

"Twin boys," she breathed.

The midwife was weeping openly and Fiona's sister seemed lost for words.

"I haven't delivered a boy in thirty years," the midwife said dabbing her eyes with a handkerchief. "Not since you were born." She looked at Matthew and he could see that she was smiling beneath her tears.

He looked at his sons. They were both so special. They were the future. He reached out and touched their soft heads.

"They're two in a million," he said.

THE CONE KEY

Caz gasped. The hybrid's nails dug into her arm, twisting, burning the skin as he tightened his grip. She shuddered yet held his gaze.

"Don't let me down," he snarled, his lips curled back, sharp canines white in the shadows.

Caz nodded. His eyes probed deep into her. What choice did she have? She nodded again and this time he released his grip and the blood flowed back into her forearm with a warm rush. For a moment those cold mustard eyes held her. And then he was gone, slipping away between the buildings and the tents towards where the obelisk rose above the village, vanishing amongst the others of his kind.

She took a slow breath, shaking, chilled to the bone despite the heat, but this was a chill of fear. Oh why hadn't she listened to the others? *Never buy anything on the black market,* they had warned her over and over in the briefings before the expedition had begun. Well she had, and now she was paying the price.

A heat haze had settled over the dig site, where canvas awnings were set up to protect them from the rage of the sun, and beneath the nearest of these Paul had stopped digging and was watching her from the shadow of his hat. She slipped back down into the pit beside him.

"What were you doing?" he hissed. "You were talking to a *throwback.*"

She didn't look at him and stooped to pick up her brush and trowel.

"They're no better than animals," he said.

Caz inspected the wall of dry earth in front of her, its surface scarred by the sweeps of her trowel. She added another to the pattern and the soil crumbled beneath her touch, dust sliding down in rivulets onto her boots.

"You shouldn't say things like that," she said, not looking round, not meeting his gaze, watching the next layer of dirt fall away. "It's racist."

At this Paul uttered a loud snort. "Racist? Ha. That would imply that they're part of the same species as us. You know they're not."

Caz didn't reply. She scraped again and paused. There was something there, just visible in the soil. She picked up the brush and swept the surface clear, dust mixing with sweat to form a thin crust on her skin. Yes, it was clearer now, glinting in the reflected light of the noonday sun. She prodded the tip on the trowel into the earth beside it and prised it loose, staring at it as it lay in the palm of her hand; a small cone shaped object only a few centimetres long, shiny and hard, perhaps made of polished stone, but its strange iridescence as she turned it over hinted at metal; a miniature replica of the obelisk that loomed above.

"Have you found something?" said Paul, his breath close to the back of her neck, and Caz slipped the object into her pocket. Perhaps this would be enough to satisfy the Hybrid?

"No, just loose stones." She scraped away the imprint the object had left and watched as the dust settled in small puffs around her boots. Paul moved away across the pit, but she could sense his eyes upon her, watching from beneath the rim of his floppy hat.

"I'm going to get a drink," she said and dropped her tools.

"That's right, leave me to do all the work," Paul mumbled as she left the shade of the awning and climbed out of the pit to walk in the full glare of the sun. She screwed up her eyes against the light, peering around the dig site as she walked. In the distance, near the village, she could see the hunched figures of a number of Hybrids milling around the market. There were normal people there too of course, but for some reason there seemed to be more Hybrids in this part of the world than she was used to. An icy chill passed up her spine, raising the fine hairs on the back of her neck. Nobody liked to say it, but they were indeed a separate species; a sub-species of humanity, a genetic split in the population. And they repulsed her. She had never dared admit it to herself before, but they did.

Beyond the village the conical shape of the obelisk rose from the desert sand. It had been there for thousands of years and nobody knew why. She touched the outside of her shorts, feeling the hard shape of the artifact in her pocket, and watched the figures in the market. And she noticed for the first time how the two species kept themselves apart. So she wasn't the only one.

Maybe she should find the Hybrid and pay him off? Maybe then he would leave her alone? Maybe nobody would notice if she slipped away now? But as she glanced round the site she could see people emerging from their pits. She stopped in her tracks. What was this? Why weren't they working?

In some of the pits further away work carried on as normal. Paul's floppy hat bobbed briefly above the edge of their pit as he shifted position, but on this side of the dig there was a buzz of excitement, a murmur of voices, and everyone was downing tools and gathering at the foot of the rock wall.

Caz frowned. Then, Hybrids forgotten, she hurried to join them.

The rock wall was a natural formation that rose like a welt, cutting through the shifting sands of the restless desert; an ancient sill of black basalt, perfect, unflawed, testimony to some ancient tectonic event that had shaped this land. Beyond the rock wall the foothills rose, barren and stark, towards the snow-capped summits of a distant range.

One of the pits had been dug at the foot of this wall and Caz joined the throngs of workers as they scrambled down into its cool depth, another awning sheltering them from the sun.

The Professor was inspecting a section of the rock wall that the excavations had exposed. It was still faintly damp, but the moist stain was fading rapidly it the dry air. Caz craned her neck to try to get a better view. There were markings on the face of the rock, faint scratchings, but not caused by the scrape of an archaeologist's trowel. The Professor was leaning down, running his hand over the rock surface and the team pressed close around him. She wormed her way forwards, pushing between the sweaty bodies of her colleagues, until at last she could see.

The rock wall was covered in writing, a scrawling script carved in a flowing hand. It was unlike anything she had ever seen.

"Unbelievable," muttered the Professor, probing with his forefinger at some sort of pit in the midst of the text. Then he stepped back, and Caz noticed something else; the professor had been inspecting a circular hole in the rock and it was about the same size as the cone she had picked up. She touched her hand to her pocket. What was this?

And then someone else was beside her in the crush, someone wearing a large floppy hat. The Professor looked up.

"Ah Paul. What do you make of this?"

Paul joined him, stroking the rock face with tenderness. "Ah yes, a very old logographic script, similar to Egyptian hieroglyphs but much more ancient. Maybe four, maybe five thousand years." He straightened up, grinning. "Give me time, I think I can work this out."

The Professor turned to the gathered crowd.

"All right everyone, back to work."

Caz melted away with the rest of them, back towards her pit. She glanced over towards the market touching the conical artifact in her pocket as she walked and her hand tingled at its touch. Maybe she wouldn't hand it over to the Hybrid just yet.

Caz rolled and fretted, but sleep wouldn't come. The sheets stuck to her sweat-soaked body and a mosquito buzzed at her from inside the net. She sighed and sat up, legs hanging over the side of her camp bed. The mosquito hummed in her ear and she slapped her hand against her neck. Silence. Then the distant hum of the desert night. There was a hint of moonlight from the world outside, just visible through the canvas of her tent. She pulled on her shorts and slipped her feet into her boots. The cone was still there, in her pocket.

Outside the tent the camp was sleeping. Distant music pulsed from the village, for the Hybrids were holding one of their ceremonies. Yet over by the rock wall a single yellow light glowed beneath the awning. Paul was still working there, late into the night. Did that man never sleep?

Caz moved in silence through the moonlight, and when she reached the pit she breathed a soft "Hello."

Paul looked up. He had dispensed with the hat and his bald head glistened silver in the moonlight. "How are you getting on?" she asked scrambling down to join him.

Paul smiled. "Not bad. Some of it is familiar enough. I've managed to start making a rough translation. Of course, it needs refining; there's always ambiguity. Words can sometimes have different meanings in different contexts, and some of them I think I've simply got wrong." He gave her a flash of crooked teeth. "Look at this."

Caz leaned forwards to look at the rock face where the light was falling. In the middle was the cone-shaped depression she had noticed earlier.

"What does it say?"

"It talks about those who are changed, and their great sacrifice. It's a description of a huge festival that was held here five thousand years ago. They believed that disaster was coming and the only way to avert it was to appease their Gods."

"Those who are changed?" Caz looked at him and he turned and caught her eye.

"I think they're talking about Hybrids."

"Hybrids? Five thousand years ago?" Caz laughed. "You've got that bit wrong. They only started to appear in the past couple of generations."

The corners of Paul's mouth creased into a sly smile.

"Do you really believe what the authorities say, that they're just a random mutation? Do you really think that the same random mutation could occur in totally separate populations throughout the world?"

Caz scowled. He had a point.

"There's an alternative theory you know: that it's a dormant gene that dates back to the dawn of mankind, and something has triggered it into activity, perhaps something environmental; perhaps it was always going to happen after a certain time."

Caz shook her head. Hybrids had been appearing throughout her life. She had never known a world without them. In some places they were killed at birth, in others sent away to be raised in institutions. She shivered. She had had a twin. They told her he had died at birth, but she had always wondered.

"What if I told you this isn't the first time," said Paul. Caz stared at him. That was crazy. But the look in his eyes was an honest one, and it wasn't his nature to tease. She shuddered. He had to be wrong.

But then his expression changed: his eyes opened wide. Caz looked up and froze. Glinting as if with their own inner light were dozens of pairs of mustard-coloured eyes, staring down from the rim of the pit.

"Hybrids," she gasped, and the distaste in her voice was clear in her ears. She hadn't heard them approach.

Then one, a larger beast, who seemed somehow in charge of this melee, climbed down into the pit beside her. Despite his bulk his movements were silent and light.

"I think you've got something for me." He held out his hand, palm red with paint, and as the light from Paul's lanterns illuminated his face she could see that it also was daubed with patterns of red. But it was a face she recognised.

"Give it to me," he said.

Caz swallowed and reached into her pocket. The cone was still there and her hand tingled at its touch, as if it was vibrating at a frequency all its own.

She handed it to the Hybrid.

"What's that?" hissed Paul. She didn't answer. "Did you take something from the dig?" He drew a sharp breath. "You did, didn't you? What have you done, Caz?"

The Hybrid held up the artifact, his mustard eyes fixed on Paul who fell silent.

"Do you know what this is?" he asked.

Paul shuffled his feet in the dirt.

"I think so. I think it's the Cone Key."

The Hybrid nodded, his mane of hair tumbling round his shoulders. "And do you know what happened here five thousand years ago?" Paul took a step back, pressing his hands against the rock wall behind him. Caz started to shake. But the Hybrid was looking at her in such an odd way, as if he was sorry for her.

"We're not going to hurt you," he said. "We're not like you *Homo sapiens*. We're not going to do what your ancestors did to us. But you can't stop evolution. This was always going to happen."

"What's he talking about?" Caz hissed to Paul. She moved closer to him, glad of the contact, glad of the human touch. The Hybrid in front of her looked taller, straighter, than he had before, as if he was their leader; their king.

"Are you going to tell her?" he said, and Paul nodded.

"Five thousand years ago," Paul's voice was high and shaky, "when our species first split, our ancestors wiped out the Hybrids – *Changed Ones* as they called them. They built this wall. Oh yes, this is no work of nature, and that cone you found is the key."

"The key to what?" She was trembling now.

"They key to what lies behind." Paul fell silent, a single tear trickling down his cheek in the moonlight.

"That's right." The Hybrid stepped forwards. He took hold of Caz's arm and ushered her to one side, yet his touch was gentle, not like the way he had held her before. Perhaps now that he had what he wanted he bore her no malice?

The cone slipped into place and the rock wall began to creak. Caz stepped back as it shifted behind her. And then, as she watched, it started to move. The wall was opening, seamless joints separating as the ages-old mechanism slid into life as though it had been made yesterday.

"What are you doing? Let me go!" A cry and scuffling at the pit edge above drew Caz's attention from the wall. The Professor was struggling, held between two Hybrids. "No!" he shouted.

But the wall was open and the Hybrid took up Paul's lantern and stepped forwards, playing the light back and forth as he did. Inside was a chamber, a vast cavern. And the floor of the cavern was littered with bones.

The Hybrid turned to face them, placing his feet with care amidst the scattered bones. Skulls stared back from hollow sockets and the shadows from the lantern flickered so that they seemed also to move.

"This is what they did," the Hybrid said holding the light up high. "This is their great sacrifice. They rounded them up, drove them in here to die and marked their grave with a cone-shaped obelisk." Then he looked up to where the Professor had finally stopped struggling. "Did you think we would not know?" His voice resonated round the cavern adding emphasis to his words. The Professor was pale. "Did you think we would not know that some of your species planned to do this same thing again? You were looking for the Cone Key weren't you?"

The Professor didn't reply.

"Five thousand years is a long time, but this act was not forgotten. It was hidden in the archives, preserved by those few of you who knew the meaning of the cone and feared we would come again. And eventually we did. But this time things are different. Not all your species is ruled by fear. Not all your species wished to see us die. And so we knew what you were doing here."

Caz looked round at Paul, and his eyes were just as shocked as hers.

The Professor though, glared down into the pit. "Do we not have a right to protect our species?" he spat.

The Hybrid stepped forward over the bones and removed the cone. The wall slid back into place behind him, until it was as it had been before, smooth rock, unblemished, natural in appearance. There was no sign of what lay beyond. Yet the images pressed in on Caz's mind and she knew she would not forget.

"It is time for a new order," said the Hybrid. "Honour the dead and leave this place. You cannot prevent the progress of evolution; you have merely delayed it by five thousand years."

Then he turned to Caz and reached out to touch her arm, and once more his touch was tender and his mustard eyes were kind.

"Accept the change," he said. "For it is not our will to hasten your extinction, but soon your species will have no choice but to step aside."

And with that he was gone, leaving the pit in a fluid movement and vanishing into the night as the Hybrids melted into the darkness. Caz stood alone with Paul at her side, the rock face behind them a shadow in the moonlight. She reached out and took hold of his hand.

A human hand.

One of the last.

THE LAST TRACES

Each step felt like flying. It was a strange sensation, drifting above the surface of the moon with every bounding stride. I sucked in dry bottled air between my teeth and grinned, squinting through tinted glass at a horizon that curved more and was closer than I was used to. The mountains were white and smooth against a pure black sky, and above was the planet; a sphere of blue and green whisked through with cloud, hanging suspended amongst the stars.

I pushed off with my booted feet once more and spread my arms as I floated back down. I wondered how long I could make these strides and my heart raced with the thrill of the strange and new. We were the first here.

I glanced round at Pirri, turning my head inside the glass bubble, and he smiled back with a flash of copper teeth, flexing his long fingers beneath the gossamer thin fabric of his nano-suit. His skin pulsed bronze and gold in his excitement.

"This is wonderful." His voice burst through the intercom and I flinched at the excessive volume. But I couldn't blame him. I felt like shouting too. To be the first to set foot on this moon – this was some honour!

Then Pirri paused and looked down at his wrist console. I saw a light reflected against his helmet; a green light flashing off and on, and when I raised my own arm I saw that mine was the same. I tapped the keypad.

"Metal," said Pirri. "Aluminium, and a small amount of titanium. It's not far from us."

I tapped a few more keys, inspecting the environmental readouts, and nodded. "There's enough left on life support. What do you think it is?"

Pirri shrugged. "There's not much. I doubt it's a natural deposit. Meteorite?"

"Could be, although I'd expect iron. Maybe it's a stony meteorite that contains some of these metals?" My heart pounded. Meteorites were my field of research. To think I might find one here – it would be perfect – untarnished by the oxidising atmosphere of the planet below. It could tell us so much about this system.

Pirri led the way, our long shadows rippling over the moon's surface as he moved. I followed, my breath short and sharp as I bit my sharp canines into my lower lip and tried to quell my excitement. It could be nothing. It could be everything.

Then Pirri paused. I could tell from the hunch of his shoulders beneath the fine fabric of his suit that it was not what he expected to see. I knew in that instant that it wasn't a meteorite and my stomach turned to lead. I drew level with him on the rocky rim of a wide valley and looked down; miles of fine dust regolith, smooth and undulating, stretching to the humps of the mountains beyond. And then I scowled and looked again, narrowing my eyes against the glare of the sunlight.

"What's that?"

"I'm not sure." Pirri started forwards, a slower pace now, skin pale amber with curiosity, and I followed, tilting my head, trying to work out what we were looking at.

"I think it's artificial," I suggested after a while. "Maybe it's one of the Elders' probes?"

"How would it end up here?"

"Hmm." He had a point. But what else could it be? It was definitely artificial, small and squat and oddly shaped. But the moment that I realised it had wheels was the same moment that I saw the footprints. I stopped dead in my tracks. Pirri, when he saw what I was staring at, stopped too. He let his breath out in a slow hiss and his face turned from amber to a pale grey-blue.

"Footprints!" I started forwards, skirting around them to leave them intact. I reached out and touched the machine.

Pirri didn't follow at first, but soon bounded over to where I was running my fingers over the machine, sensing the metal through my nano-suit.

"Do you know what this means?" he said, and a shiver passed through my skin.

I nodded. "We're not the first after all."

"The Elders must have landed here when they first came," said Pirri. "But why didn't they tell us? I thought we were to be the first. I thought they ignored the moon and went straight to the planet." His face deepened to blue with disappointment.

But my heart was racing. This couldn't be.

"Pirri," I said. "Look again. This isn't our technology. These aren't the footprints of our people. Someone was here all right, but not one of us."

I shivered again as I spoke and looked around at the rolling white hills. These footprints were so fresh looking that they could have been made yesterday. But in the vacuum of space they could have been here for millions of years, with no atmosphere to stir the dust and no wind to winnow them away. When I looked closer at the metal of the machine I saw the tiny pockmarks from the bombardment of minute particles of space dust on this atmosphere-less world.

These things had indeed been here a very long time. I let out a slow breath of relief. For a moment I had feared that whoever had made those footprints might still be here.

"Are you suggesting that we're not the only space-faring people?" Pirri's face was mauve with incredulity, his eyes wide despite the brilliance of the sun. He flexed his long thin fingers as he spoke. "How come we've never come across them before?"

I shrugged for I had no answer. I pointed towards the footprints. "Bipeds," I said. "And this machine would seem to be some sort of wheeled transport device. There appears to be a seat. This will tell us a fair bit about their size and shape." I scowled. "The technology is pretty basic for interstellar travellers," I murmured.

Pirri wandered away from me, following the footprints. "Look, there's something here." He stooped and picked it up. "Some sort of plaque covered in what I guess must be a form of writing." He held it up for me to see. "And a little figure. Perhaps it's what they look like?"

I scowled at the writing, which was unlike anything I'd seen produced even by the more advanced races our people had encountered. The figure was rudimentary, impressionistic. The machine could tell us more.

"Let's see what else we can find," I said.

It was Pirri who found the next artifact. He let out a whoop of excitement and turned towards me holding up another plaque.

"A map of their world!" His face pulsed gold.

I bounded over for a closer look. It was indeed a map. I frowned. There was something about that map, the way some of the pieces of continent seemed to fit, although they were closer than they should be.

"What's wrong," said Pirri. "You're showing lilac."

"I'd quite like to show this to Dil," I said.

Pirri laughed. "What? That lunatic!" Then he frowned orange. "Why?"

"I think it's a map of the planet, before it was mostly covered with ice, before the continents drifted so far apart."

"Maybe it is," said Pirri, the gold flush glowing once more. "Maybe it's what the planet looked like when they came here."

I smiled at him. "Of course, you're right." But in my heart was a strange disquiet.

I paused on the gallery and looked down over the railing at the floor below and the figure hurrying towards the exit. It was Dil, a shawl pulled round his bare shoulders, and his skin pulsed red with defiance. I clasped the railing, cold beneath my fingers and leaned forwards for a better look. Where was he going so near to sunset? I still wanted to talk to him, although I knew that to do so would bring down the wrath of the Elders. We were not supposed to mention the artifacts we had found to anybody.

I glanced at my wrist console. The debrief was over for today and was due to resume in the morning, and I was tired. But there was something about Dil's colour and the way he walked. What was he up to? And he walked like the Dil I had known of old, before they discredited him.

I swallowed, and when I looked down at my hands I saw that my own skin pulsed red as well. I was going to follow, and it seemed that my skin knew this even before I admitted it to myself.

Outside the domes I paused, blinking in the last of the light. The distant mountains formed jagged silhouettes against the setting sun and the chill breeze of evening stroked my bare skin. In the distance the fields were quiet, the harvesters stilled for the night and the workers had gone to wherever it was they went at dusk. I shuddered. This wasn't a good time of day to be out here alone.

Dil's red glow was moving along the track towards the trees and I narrowed my eyes. If I didn't move fast I would lose him in the woods, and I set off after him, never taking my eyes off his crimson light, my feet heavy and clumsy after the lightness of space.

Soon the dark canopy closed over my head and the path narrowed to a dusty track. I blinked and squinted into the gloom. Darkness came quickly in the forest, but I could still see Dil's light up ahead. And then I tripped.

I've no idea what it was – a root, a stone? One moment I was striding along and the next I was face down in the dirt with a mouthful of grit. I rolled over and the trees spun above me, dark branches obscuring an indigo sky. A few stars winked at me through the canopy, and when I stood up there was no other light. Dil had vanished and my own glow had faded to the dull grey of fear. I blinked but could see nothing.

I started to creep forwards, feeling the ground with my feet, holding my hands in front of me, testing for obstruction. My eyes strained against the black. Why was I doing this? I should be at home awaiting tomorrow's debrief. I shouldn't be chasing after Dil. Our friendship was over, forgotten. I should leave it that way.

The ground was uneven now and I stumbled. Either the path had gone or I had strayed. I paused. I should go back. But when I turned I had no idea which way 'back' should be. I couldn't see the sky to orientate myself. I gulped down my fear.

And then I heard movement. I wasn't alone.

I froze, hoping they wouldn't know I was here, my eyes struggling to see. These forests were full of wild creatures, some savage and dangerous. But whatever these were they knew I was here. From the rustle of leaves and occasional snap of a twig I could tell they were coming closer. I shuddered and cursed my foolishness.

Then they were all around me, touching me, testing, and my flesh recoiled in horror at the alien contact.

I blinked and for a moment I could see their eyes, purple with reflected light. There was light on the trunks of the trees as well, and I could see them, their hunched stature and coarse manes of hair –

Primitives! I cowered away from their touch. And then they were gone, a scuffle of leaves and they vanished into the undergrowth.

I looked around at the source of the light, and my glow of green relief mixed with the light from the figure standing between the trees.

"Dil," I gasped.

The figure gave a flash of pink surprise at the sound of my voice.

"You?" The pink merged into red. "What are you doing out here? It's dangerous."

"I saw you leaving the domes. I was wondering…"

"I hear you've been on the moon," Dil said.

I faltered. "Yes, yes I have."

"So why did you follow me?" There was an edge of bitterness to his voice. I swallowed.

"I'm sorry Dil, I'm sorry about everything that happened."

"And?"

"And there's something I need to talk to you about."

The red tinge to his skin ebbed to orange. "Something about the moon?"

"Yes." My voice was barely a whisper.

"And of course the Elders don't know you're here?"

"No."

Dil smiled and his orange hue pulsed to amber. "You'd better follow me."

He led the way between the trees. Now the forest was full of sounds, insects chirping in the night and small creatures scurrying away as we passed, but they no longer threatened. When I glanced up I saw that the canopy had thinned and the sky had lightened with the moonrise. Occasional bats darted between the branches – fleeting silhouettes. With Dil beside me my earlier fears evaporated. He walked with confidence, without fear. He knew this place.

In time we came to the edge of the forest and looked out across a broad beach; sand silver in the moonlight, and the waves breaking on the shore gave off a faint phosphorescent glow.

It was the fire that drew my eye and I stepped back into the shelter of the trees. Flames blazed and sparks rose into the sky to vanish in the night. Yet it was the creatures around it that made my flesh crawl; one of the higher forms native to this world, but animals none the less.

"Dil!" I hissed, but Dil just laughed.

"Come on." He started forwards but stopped and turned when I did not follow.

"They've got a fire!" I hissed.

Dil grinned and his skin turned yellow. "That's right."

"But how?"

"They made it. Come on. They won't hurt us." He turned towards the fire.

This time I followed, trying to walk in silence, every instinct screaming at me to leave. I didn't want to go anywhere near these creatures, a species that I had only ever seen from a distance. They were harmless, but of no use to us. Not like the others that we used to work the land, or the creatures I had just encountered that I would rather forget.

Dil walked straight up to them and they stopped what they were doing and turned to stare, their eyes turning to me, scanning me up and down. My skin squirmed beneath their gaze, yellow eyes above broad muzzles.

One of them moved aside to make a space on the log upon which it was squatting, balancing itself with its broad tail. Dil sat down, running his hand over the smooth fur of its head. It half closed its eyes and a soft growl rumbled in its throat.

I stood on the edge of the firelight, stretching my long fingers. The night chill had settled on the forest and I yearned for the warmth of that fire, yet I dared go no closer. Dil turned and beckoned me over but when I shook my head he turned away, and the creatures turned away as well as I stood and watched, bemused.

One of their number was crouching on its haunches by the fire, waving its arms in rhythm with the strange guttural sounds it was uttering. The others sat in silence, watching it, eyes fixed, enthralled.

And Dil was watching too.

After a few minutes I started to creep closer. The creatures didn't seem to notice, and there was something hypnotic about the rhythm of the speaker's voice. The fire spat, drowning out its grunts, and sparks jetted into the air. The others leaned forwards as if trying better to hear.

I joined Dil on his log, lowering myself to sit beside him. He turned to me and smiled.

"What are they doing?" I hissed.

"Listening." He was still stroking the creature beside him and it half opened its eyes to look at me, then closed them again.

"Listening?" I asked. "To what?"

"It's an ancient legend."

"What?" I turned to look at the creature by the fire, the rapt expressions on the onlooker's faces, and then back to Dil. "Can you understand them?" I asked.

Dil nodded.

"What are they saying?"

"It's an ancient legend." Dil's voice was barely a whisper. "I've heard it told before but this one tells it particularly well. It tells of a time when there was only one moon in the sky – a constant moon that did not change, a moon that was always full. But then the second moon came and sang a song of the first moon's love for the sun and the first moon was ashamed for she had been hiding her feelings for so long. So now she runs before the sun and hides her face from him, and only when she is alone in the sky will she shine in her glory, before running to hide once more."

I stared at him and then at the orator who was still speaking, oblivious to Dil's whispering.

"He speaks of us?" I turned back to Dil and he nodded.

"He does indeed. The second moon is quite clearly the ship that brought the Elders here, two hundred years ago and still up there. To these creatures it would appear as a second moon."

"But that's amazing. That they should remember!"

Dil smiled. "This species is evolving fast. They have fire and language and the more time I spend with them the more I realise that they have a very complex social structure. They also have this strong oral tradition."

"Is that why you're here? Are you studying their legends?"

Dil smiled. "I think that there might be some substance to their tales, so, yes."

"And you think they might support your theories."

For a moment Dil's colour faltered and the creature beside him opened its eyes to stare at me.

"You know me better than I know myself," said Dil. But I was staring at the creature beside him, for there was something in its eyes that was more than just a pet being stroked. I saw that it was female and it had feelings too – feelings that I had never, before that moment thought that animals such as these could have. And I wondered if Dil could see it too.

Dil and his theories – he'd been discredited – couldn't he see that? His ideas were quite plainly wrong. But I looked at the speaker beside the fire and the female purring at Dil's touch and I wondered.

The speaker finished his tale and some of the creatures moved off into the sea to dance in the phosphorescent waves, and Dil's female went with them. We sat together on the log and I watched the firelight playing through the embers.

"So why did you come?" Dil asked after a while, and suddenly it was as if we were friends again, as of old, and nothing had ever happened. And maybe I could mend what I had done, for it was I who had caused his downfall.

"We found something on the moon," I said. "I wanted to show you."

For a moment Dil's skin pulsed faster. "Did you?"

"Look." I held out my arm and tapped my wrist console with my fingers to project the holographic image into the space before us. One of the creatures whimpered and crept away at the sight and those others that were still around the fire watched in silence with curious eyes.

"This is the transport device we found," I said as the first image hovered in the air.

Dil blinked. "Look at those footprints – maybe one, maybe two individuals. That transport device looks rather primitive."

I smiled. "Yes, I know. But that's not what the Elders are saying."

"Oh?"

"And this is the figure we found, and the first plaque."

Dil leaned forwards for a better look. "A curious script."

"Have you ever seen anything like that?"

"No, never." Dil scratched his arm and his skin assumed a puzzled orange.

"And this is the second plaque."

"Ah," Dil reached forwards as if to touch the image, but remembered and withdrew his hand at the last moment. He turned to me and his eyes were bright, his skin golden once more. "More of that script," he said. "And a map."

I nodded.

"So what do the Elders want you to say?"

I smiled, same old Dil, always the rebel, always looking for a conspiracy. But this time he was right.

"At first they wanted to say that it must have been our ancestors who visited the moon after all, despite all the records which tell that they passed it by as a barren rock and came straight to the planet."

"But it's pretty obvious it isn't," said Dil. I switched off the console and lowered my arm.

"Then they decided that it must be another space-faring race that visited that moon in the distant past. After all, those relics and those footprints could have been there for millions of years."

"That much is true," said Dil. "But the species that built that machine didn't have the technology for interstellar travel."

"They say that the map shows the world from which they came."

Dil snorted. "And what do you say?"

I smiled. So Dil could see it too. "Well if you imagine those continents a little further apart, and then cover most of the northern and southern hemispheres with ice the way the world is now then, well, it's this world the map is showing. This world as it must have been millions of years ago, before the ice came."

I was almost breathless as I finished, looking up at Dil as I had back then, the pupil staring at the teacher, yearning for approval. Dil nodded and the glow of his skin showed that I was right.

"So it proves that your theories are correct?"

Dil shrugged. "Perhaps." The embers reflected in his eyes as the creatures that had been romping in the waves returned to the fire to groom and dry their fur in the warmth. Dil looked across at them.

"Incredible aren't they," he said. "They've evolved so far so fast, language, fire, folklore. As I study their language and their society the more I admire them. This world is ready for a higher species, a greater intelligence that that which it possesses now."

"But you can't mean – not them."

Dil laughed. "No, of course not. This is a new species, recently evolved. But maybe in a few million years they might advance enough to develop space flight."

"But you still think that whatever made those footprints and left those artifacts must have come from this world and not from another."

"The technology they have could only have permitted travel within this solar system. None of the other planets contain life, so the only solution is that they came from this one."

I straightened up and grinned, my whole body pulsing with delight. So I was right. I knew it!

"So do you have any evidence for this?" I asked.

But Dil shook his head. "Perhaps there was once, but if there was a civilisation on this world all traces of it have been scraped away by the ice."

I sighed. "And they became extinct when their world changed. Such is the fate we see so often, for those species that never made it to the stars."

"Perhaps they became extinct, perhaps not."

I turned and stared at Dil, biting back the urge to laugh. He was serious.

"What other species on this world could possibly have been to the moon? They are all just animals."

"Try the Primitives."

I shuddered and my skin turned icy blue at the thought, those animals in the forest, crowding round me, touching, sharp teeth and ragged manes of hair. I pulled a face.

"They are just animals."

"They are now. And soon they will vanish into oblivion when our friends here," and he nodded towards the creatures by the fire, "finally supersede them. Yet for now they cling on."

I stared at the creatures by the fire. The female smoothed her whiskers and looked up at Dil. Then she moved across to join us once more.

"The Elders won't accept this," I said in a whisper. "The Primitives are vermin, to be treated as such. To suggest that they may have once been civilised will be unthinkable. They're not going to like it when I tell them."

"I know that," said Dil.

I looked across at him, the golden glow of his skin reassuring. He belonged here, with these creatures. And he didn't mind what I had done, all those years ago.

# #

"That's all of them," said Pirri as he tossed the last of the space debris into the lunar transport. He pulsed with the multicolours of satisfaction and flashed his copper teeth in a grin. I glanced up at the planet, blue and serene, then back down at the footprints, traces aeons old where once the Primitive's ancestors had walked across this empty landscape, their first faltering steps into space, steps that had gone no further.

I tightened my grip on the brush, then swept it across the fine regolith as were my orders, obliterating those footprints for all time.

No one now would ever know.

THE CURSED ZOO

The house was impressive by any standards, arches and turrets, approached by a wide sweeping drive. There were manicured lawns and sculpted shrubs, and a white marble statue poured down water into a pond, casting iridescent rainbows in the sunlight. I reined in my horse and stared. The Crown Prince certainly kept his mistresses in style.

The horse fretted his bit and tossed his head, his hide flecked white with the spume of his sweat. I patted his damp neck and I sensed his unease through my legs. He wasn't the only one. The scent of death surrounded this place like fog. I urged him forwards.

There was a man waiting for me at the top of the wide flight of steps that led to the front door, a burly man with a burgundy waistcoat and matching cravat. I could tell by his officious stance and the wary look in his eyes that he must be the policeman in charge of this case. I sighed. They always looked at me that way.

He shoved his thumbs into his waistcoat pockets and scowled as I handed my horse over to a groom and marched up the steps to stand before him. I swept my cloak around me with a flourish and tipped my hat, but I didn't offer him my hand to shake. I knew he wouldn't take it. It was plain to see that he resented my presence. His kind always did.

"The Agency sent me," I said, as if I needed to tell him – the mere sight of me was enough – and he grunted in acknowledgement. "Which way is the body?"

For a moment he glared at me, open hostility. But then he mustered control over his features and shrugged and turned. "This way." He led me inside.

She was lying in the hallway at the foot of the staircase, her legs twisted under her, her head at an odd angle, hair a mass of bleached blonde curls and too much rouge upon her cheeks. But the teeth marks on her throat told me everything I needed to know – that and the strange lack of blood at the scene of her death. Oh, the folly of the rich: their vanity and greed, their desire to possess that which they could not control.

"Did they catch it?" I asked.

The policeman nodded. "They did more than that." He gave me such a stony glare that it would have withered me, had I been human.

"Show me."

"Hmph." He led me through a ballroom of mirrors and crystal chandeliers, and out onto the wide stone terrace, before which stretched the lake, glinting in the sunlight. A gentleman with a tweed cloak and a monocle stood waiting, leaning against the balustrade, his shoulders hunched and his face downturned. By his feet lay the creature.

I squatted beside it, but didn't reach out to touch. Its skin had faded to the dull grey of death, its lips curled back to reveal the triple row of teeth. I sighed. Why did the super-rich want to keep such savage beasts as pets? It was something about these people that I would never understand.

"Did you kill it?" I asked, and the gentleman before me nodded. His eyes didn't hold the same hatred for my kind that the policeman's did, but they were shadowed with sorrow. "The lady?"

"The Countess was my sister."

"And this?" I gestured towards the dead creature between us.

"I told her it was a bad idea. But would she listen? It's all the rage at court these days. They try to outdo each other with their exotic pets. Her cousin has a snow leopard. I think she was trying to better her with this…" He gestured with his hand towards the prone shape, fierce even in death, and this was just a cub! "This… thing."

I nodded and rose to my feet. "I'll get rid of it for you."

"Good."

"Just one thing."

He looked up at me and his eyes were shining with restrained tears. The grief he clearly felt but was too proud to show.

"Where did she get it from?"

He lowered his eyes once more and shrugged. "I do not know for sure. She spoke of a man, a dealer in exotic animals. They all talk of him.

He commands a high price and his clients are Barons and Queens. His service is said to be discrete but the rarity and splendour of the beasts unsurpassed."

I had heard it all before.

"Does he bring them in?"

"I'm not sure." He turned away from me, leaning on the parapet, staring out across the lake.

I had one more question.

"Can you give me a name?"

I had him now. There was no escape. I pushed him back, hard against the wall of the barn, staring into his eyes and he cowered beneath my gaze. His greased back hair had flopped forwards onto his face and his skin was stretched thin over his gaunt features, the faint tinge of purple bruising already beginning to show. A trickle of blood ran from his nose. I didn't regret hitting him.

"Tell me what you know?"

He twisted beneath my grasp but I tightened my grip. His shirt tore, fabric and stitches ripping apart. At that sound his struggles ceased. His eyes narrowed and a fine sweat beaded his forehead but still he did not reply. The scent of his fear was stronger.

"Speak," I demanded and dug my fingernails into his flesh. He winced and half parted his lips, his breath stale with beer, his teeth crooked, yellow.

But it was a different voice that spoke. "You won't find your answers with him."

I turned at the sound of the voice but held my captive firm. The innkeeper had joined us, here, behind the stables, ruddy cheeks showing through his whiskers.

"And what would you know of my business?" I asked.

"I know why you are here," he said, a smile on his lips but not in his eyes. "I know what you are."

"You know nothing about me," I said, clenching my fingers into my captive's neck and he grunted and gagged at my strangling grip. "Leave me to do my work."

"That man is of no use to you. He is merely a go-between. It is he who strikes the deals. You seek another man. A man like you."

"Like me?"

I looked once more into the fear-filled eyes of the man in my clasp and he lowered his head in a nod. So that was why he would not speak. I was not the only one he feared. So it was one of my own kind that he was dealing with. I might have known.

I flung him aside and down. He struggled in the dirt on his hands and knees, coughing in the dust and dung. Then he glanced up at me and scrambled to his feet, mud-smeared britches and ragged shirt. He rubbed at his neck with one hand and steadied himself against the wall of the barn. Then he lurched away from us, vanishing back towards the inn and the solace of a tankard of beer.

I stepped towards the innkeeper.

"Tell me what you know."

He looked at me and his eyes were calm.

"I am not afraid of you. I was a boy when your people arrived. I saw the lights in the sky and heard the whispers in the shadows. Beer loosens men's tongues, and the tongues of your kind are no different."

I stared at him. So others came here to this inn. But who, and why?

"And what do you hear?" I asked.

"I hear of extraction plants out in the ocean. I hear that you came here for salt."

I nodded. "You hear correctly."

"I also hear that you will only take what you need, and we on this planet will never notice it has gone. I hear that you go to great pains that the ways of our people should not be disturbed. You see yourselves as guests on this world. People are afraid of you but they need not be."

His smile broadened, parting his whiskers to show tombstone teeth, stained ochre from chewing tobacco.

"You are right," I said, "and that is why I am here. There are those who seek to make a quick profit; influences that should not be allowed to infiltrate your people, things that should not be brought in."

"Like the trafficking of exotic beasts," said the innkeeper and his smile at last reached his eyes.

"Yes." My voice was barely a whisper. I wanted to reach out and grab him and shake the knowledge from his lips. He was toying with me. But I could also see that he was going to tell me without coercion, so I stayed my hand.

"You are closer than you know," he said. "Up in the hills, in the forest, is a lake, the Black Lake. I see the lights of the sky ships descending in the dead of night. That is where they bring them in. We call it the Cursed Zoo."

I stared at him. "Thank you," I said, and was about to take my leave. But then I noticed that the smile had vanished from his eyes and lips as if a dark shadow had passed across his face. His scent changed with his mood. There was something else; something he hadn't told me. Yet.

"There is more?" It was a statement of fact as much as a question.

"Yes, there is more."

"Then speak."

He took a deep breath. "There is something going on in those woods. The lights came some weeks ago, but this time they never left. I have several regular guests who stop here as they pass though on their way from the forest villages. But in the past week my customers have grown fewer."

He paused, scuffing the toe of one boot in the dirt, then stooped to pick up a coin that someone had dropped. He turned it over in his hand and slipped it into his pocket. He turned his gaze back to me. "And then the man you were speaking to just now came back. He had been trading in Vienna; a wealthy client. I read about it in the papers. The Countess?"

"Yes," I said, my voice cold. "The Countess."

The innkeeper nodded. "He was returning to the forest, to the Cursed Zoo. But I have told him not to go. They are up to something and it is not good."

And now his eyes were alight.

"You know why I tell you this?" he said.

I stepped away from him, staring up at the mountain range beyond the inn, the blue haze of fir trees in the evening light.

"You want me to go and find this man, and this Cursed Zoo."

"Yes," he said. "Find this man and find out why he had blockaded the forest. It is in both our interests. You do understand that my motives are selfish. This Cursed Zoo is bad for business."

And for the first time in the company of a human, I smiled.

# #

It had rained overnight and the forest was dripping, large drops thumping into the damp earth and pine needles. Apart from that, and the sound of my horse's hooves, this forest was silent; no birds, no insects, nothing. Just the wind and patterns of sunlight and shade cast between the branches of the trees.

The lake was ahead, the smell of water and rotting vegetation catching in my throat. The Cursed Zoo was near.

The horse tossed his head and jangled his bit, stepping to one side as if to shy and run. I patted his neck to soothe his nerves.

"It's just a forest," I said, and he flicked his ears back at the sound of my voice, but did not cease his fidgeting. And then we walked into it; the Cursed Zoo. But it was deserted.

I swore beneath my breath and dismounted. I looped the reins around a branch and strode into the centre of the clearing, sweeping my cloak around me and taking my hat from my head to run my fingers over my smooth scalp. I stood and stared around.

The Cursed Zoo had been large, a far larger operation than I had expected. There were cages all around the clearing, some on the ground and others elevated into the branches of the trees. All were made of branches and forest wood, specially reinforced, and all were empty. Those I was seeking had gone. They had taken their trade elsewhere.

And this was no small trade. This was on a scale unlike anything I had seen before – a large scale importing business – the trafficking of exotic species from other worlds. Totally illegal – totally against everything our species stood for. They risked contamination of this planet's fragile ecosystem – and all in the name of greed and vanity.

My search had come to a dead end. The death of the Countess must have warned them. They would have known that I would follow their trail and find them here. And so they had gone. I was too slow. I was going to have to seek elsewhere.

I took a deep breath and turned back to my horse. He was pulling back, straining at his reins. His eyes rolled showing their whites and froth foamed at his mouth. Fresh sweat glistened on his hide. I stopped, scowling, and then I smelt it: Death.

I pulled my cloak close and looked around. I could see nothing but the scent was growing stronger, a light breeze picking up and fanning it in off the lake. But this time the scent wasn't human. It was the scent of my own kind.

So they hadn't left after all.

All around the clearing the forest started to move; it came alive as they closed in. I looked around, my eyes frantic, my breath sharp gasps. But everywhere I looked there were more. What folly was this? How many of these creatures had these people brought into this world?

Fear gripped me, clutching my heart, choking my breath.

And then I saw what I had not noticed before – not all the cages had been properly reinforced, and on those that were not broken the locks had been shattered and bore the marks of teeth and claws. How blinded they must have been by riches and greed? They knew the dangers of this species, and yet they had made do with cages that could not hold. They should have known better.

The creatures circled round me, their colours changing with their background. Three rows of teeth. It would at least be quick

The horse strained back and the reins snapped as he pulled away. But before he could run the forest around him came to life. A creature leaped up from the thickets and brush and onto the horse before he had a chance to flee, its skin at first the colour of pine leaves and patterned like bark, and then the brown of the horse itself; a brown that changed to red as it brought him down onto his knees with three rows of teeth in his jugular vein. For the first time on this planet I heard a horse cry out in fear.

It was his screams made me move. I shook off the torpor that consumed me and turned and ran. The creatures did not follow and I ran until I thought my heart would burst, the death screams of my horse echoing in my ears long after he had fallen.

The creatures did not follow but still I ran.

I was too late. There were now monsters loose upon this world.

In the Precinct of Amun-Re

The hot air enveloped Inez like a shroud as she stepped from the air-conditioned chill of the hotel lobby into the bustling street. She paused on the steps to adjust her hat and sunglasses and glanced around, her breath shallow as the heat smothered her – and yet it was still only early. She knew by midday it would be almost unbearable. It was the worst time of year to have come, but she couldn't have waited.

The street before her was bustling with activity, shops selling spices and ornate perfume bottles, men drinking tea and playing backgammon in the doorways. A youth brandishing a scroll of fake papyrus spotted her and began to approach, and Inez moved away. She wasn't looking for souvenirs.

At the far end of the street was the Nile, the distinctive sails of the wooden fellucas passing by. She could smell the dry heat and the spices from the stalls that she passed and the hubbub of voices blurred into background noise.

She flipped open her guidebook and ran her fingers over the postcard that marked her place – the city of Luxor, ancient Thebes, Karnak and the valley of the kings. The postcard held few clues; the picture was the typical montage of a few of the more famous tourist sites and on the back was written the words '*Join me. Alonzo x,*' in her brothers distinctive sloping scrawl.

She turned it over in her hand, looking first at the pictures then at his message, then at the pictures once more. This was the first contact from him in five years. But now she was here she had no idea how to find him and all she could think to do was visit the sites in the picture, hoping.

She set off once more, purpose in her stride, her destination decided. She had visited the Valley of the Kings the previous day, crossing the Nile on the vast floating raft that served as a ferry, being followed by a small boy in a long green robe until at last she relented and bought the carved stone scarab he held out to her. She had felt the venom of the unrelenting desert sun beating back off the bare rock, and descended into the choking stuffiness of the tombs, marvelling at the detail of the carving on the sarcophagi and the beauty of the paintings on the walls. But she had returned to the hotel alone.

Today she would visit the next postcard scene.

She arrived at the temple of Karnak and followed a group of Japanese tourists in through the entrance, rapid chatter and clicking cameras, past the armed guard who watched them pass from beneath bushy brows. Once inside they spread out and Inez moved away from them, pausing by a stone ram-sphinx to study the entry in her book.

"Hello Inez." The voice made her jump, for she hadn't realized anyone was standing so nearby. She looked up swiftly, feeling her pulse quicken. She had been hoping for this, but hadn't dared believe. "I've been waiting for you," said Alonzo.

Inez smiled. He was dressed in typical Egyptian clothes, his face more tanned and perhaps a little thinner, but otherwise looking much the same as he had when he had left to go travelling five years ago.

"How could I have ignored this," she said lifting the postcard for him to see. Then she put it back in the guidebook. "So is this where you've been all this time?"

Alonzo shook his head, and she noticed that his black hair seemed to be oiled. He stroked the ram's head, almost with affection.

"No," he said. "Not here."

"Well where then? And why didn't you write – or call – anything?" She flinched at the sound of her voice. She wanted to take him in her arms and hold him tight and tell him how much she had missed her little brother, but something in his demeanour held her back. He seemed different and it frightened her. And all she could do was shout at him!

"I couldn't. Not where I was," he said, looking at the ground, not meeting her gaze.

"You've been in prison, haven't you?" she raged. "You've done something awful. But you still should have called. I thought you were dead!" She felt tears welling up behind her eyes and blinked them back.

But the anger was fading. "I'm sorry Alonzo, I was so worried. You're all I have. You still should have called. It wouldn't have mattered. So were you in prison?"

Alonzo shook his head again. "No, I was elsewhere." He looked up at last, meeting her gaze. "I'll explain as we walk. Let me show you around."

He led her slowly past high statues and crumbling walls. "We are in the great forecourt of the precinct of Amun-Re, he said.

"It says that much in my guidebook."

"Ah, but I can show you a few things that are not in any guidebook." He grinned at her, his teeth white against the scorched brown of his skin. "Follow me to the temple of Rameses the third."

"That's in my guidebook too." Inez lifted the book and used it to fan herself as she followed him across the precinct. The heat was building as the sun rose, beating down on her and blasting back as the earth and stone around her reflected its anger. Already the clusters of tourists were seeking out the shade.

"It's beautiful here, isn't it?" He paused in front of a frieze depicting a massacre whilst the gods looked on. "You can almost feel the past. Close your eyes. It's as if you can reach out and touch them." Inez scowled at him and he laughed.

"They're closer than you think," he hissed, and it was Inez's turn to laugh.

"It's good to see you again, Alonzo. Are you staying near here?"

"You could say that," he said with a flash of white teeth as they moved on round the temple. "Close your eyes."

"Why?"

"Do it."

Inez obliged.

"Now listen, what do you hear?"

Inez listened to the sounds; the chatter of tourists moving amongst the ruins, the sound of their shoes on the stone, the click of their cameras. She almost imagined that she could hear the sun beating back at her from the stone and the ground cracking in the heat.

"You can hear them can't you," said Alonzo, his voice hushed as if he was afraid of being overheard. "They are moving towards the altar, there's a white calf waiting for them, a golden orb set between its horns. Can you smell its sweat? Can you hear their voices? They are carrying incense and its scent permeates the temple. The odour is heady and intoxicating. They are chanting. Do you hear what they are saying?"

For a moment Inez could almost smell the incense and hear the sounds of the high priest's chants. She giggled and opened her eyes.

Alonzo was smiling at her. "Come on, let me show you the hypostyle hall."

He led the way back across the precinct where the sun glared down at them from a vivid sky, and Inez was glad when they moved into a pool of shade between high walls.

"The great hypostyle hall." Alonzo swept his arms with a flourish as they passed through the second pylon. "Built by Rameses the second over three thousand years ago." He wandered between the columns and Inez stared up dizzily as she walked. The columns were completely covered in hieroglyphics, every space inscribed. On the outer walls of the hall, towards which Alonzo led her, the writing was interspersed with magnificent relief friezes, depictions of battles, ceremonies and loved ones of a civilisation now crumbling into dust.

Alonzo paused in front of one of these. "What do you think of this chap?" he said, turning his head sideways and striking a pose, imitating the carved figure before him. The Japanese tourist who had been staring at the frieze moved away.

Inez laughed. "He could be your twin," she said. "I always thought you had an odd-shaped face."

Alonzo gave her a sideways glance, then looked back at the figure. "That's because this is me," he said. "This is the day I came before Rameses. The day I told him how he could save his city."

Inez laughed out loud. "Course it is, Alonzo. But you'd better watch out 'cos there's a bandage dragging mummy following us."

Alonzo frowned. "Don't mock me, Inez. This is important."

"Oh I see. You weren't in prison at all. You've escaped from a mental hospital."

"You know that's not true." He moved over to the nearest column and ran his fingers over the detailed carved inscriptions. "See this symbol."

Inez followed him. "Yes, it's a cartouche. It's the name of someone important, a pharaoh or a god."

"It's my name," he said, looking at her with a strange intensity in his eyes. Something squirmed up Inez's spine and she shifted her sandaled feet uneasily, feeling the dry dust coating her skin. "And this one," he added reaching towards another, different cartouche, "is yours."

"Don't be ridiculous. Why would anyone have written our names in an Egyptian temple three thousand years ago?"

"Because I told them to. Because I was there."

Inez drew a deep breath. "Okay Alonzo. You're acting really freaky. Can we just finish the tour and go and get something to eat, and have a proper talk."

Alonzo gave his head a gentle shake.

"There isn't time," he said staring at her, his eyes ablaze. "Did you ever wonder where we came from, our parents – our real parents?"

"I'm not interested in finding my real parents. I'm quite happy the way I am. But I take it you went looking."

"I did," said Alonzo. "And you know what – they don't exist. Not in this time anyway."

Inez opened her mouth to say something reassuring to him, but hesitated, for his eyes had dulled suddenly and he seemed somehow gaunt and strained, as if all the troubles of the world weighed down on his shoulders.

"This place is special. This is a joining place, shifting in and out of phase. The ancients knew this. That is why they built their temple here. It's a regular and predictable event, but the openings are small and localised and only last a few seconds. It'll be in phase soon and you'll be able to go through."

"What *are* you talking about? Go through where?"

He raised his eyes to meet hers and the fire had returned, a burning passion, or maybe madness. He stepped forwards and took hold of her arms, his fingers digging into her skin. She gasped at the tightness of his grip.

"You and I are out of time Inez. That is why I could not find our parents. My place is with Rameses, my Pharaoh. But you Inez, you have a far greater destiny. Thebes is going to be destroyed and only you can turn back the evil, only you can save the city."

Inez stared at him, feeling small beads of sweat trickle down her spine. Her breath came in short gasps and she didn't dare speak. He had pushed his face up close to her and she could feel his breath. Then he broke away and pointed up at the cartouche he had shown her.

"Look Inez, there is your name, a cry for help from three thousand years ago."

"You're crazy," hissed Inez rubbing her arms. "All this talk of parallel worlds…"

"No." Alonzo was standing in front of her again. He seemed somehow taller, more domineering. "Just time; a phase shift in time. You will go through. You will save Thebes. In just a few minutes the shift will align again, just briefly, and the window will be small. I am here to show you the way."

"But what makes you think I can do anything?" she gasped.

"Because it is written. Rameses showed me the texts. They described my arrival at his palace exactly how it happened, and as I read them I realised that they were talking about you as well."

"Even if I believed you, how am I supposed to save the city?" she said, feeling herself shrinking away from him, resisting the urge to run. He really was crazy.

"You will know; it is in your heart. They will rally behind you. They will rise up." He smiled and for a moment it was her brother of old before her. "You will not fail." Then the look of tenderness was gone and his eyes were full of fire and rage once more. "It is time."

He took hold of her hand and dragged her along behind him through the hall, between the tall columns that passed in a blur. Inez could feel his nails digging into her wrist as she stumbled over the uneven floor. Her heart was thumping and she had started to shake.

At last he stopped and turned to face her. "This is it." His voice seemed to echo. In front of her, Inez could see the air between two of the columns shimmering. She blinked. It was like a heat haze, a mirage in a desert of stone. Alonzo was staring at her.

"Are you ready?"

"No. This is crazy, you're crazy. This is all wrong! I can't go back in time to save a city that never fell. It doesn't make sense."

Alonzo didn't appear to have heard. He reached into his pocket and pulled something out, a pendant, and he looped the chain over her head.

"I nearly forgot," he said with a smile. "You'll be needing that. So they know it's you." Inez held the pendant in her hand and glanced down at it, a single eye staring back from lacquer and gold. Then his hands were on her shoulders and he was pushing her forwards.

Inez gasped and strained back, leaning into him, but he was too strong for her. She was in the mirage and it was cold. Her vision blurred as the chill caressed her skin, making the hairs stand up on end. She stepped forwards, back into the heat, and her vision cleared.

She was still there, in the great hypostyle hall, but it was now night. In front of her were people dressed in long robes. When they saw her they fell to their knees, and she knew they had been waiting for her. The hall was lit by burning brands, mounted on the columns. They cast flickering shadows, which made the carved figures appear to move. But the columns were not new. This place was still a ruin. She looked up at a dark sky of billowing smoke and then realised that beyond she could see the city, but it wasn't the Luxor she knew. It was a vast city of skyscrapers, concrete and glass, and it was on fire. This city was burning, laid to waste; this was the city she was meant to have saved.

For this wasn't the past. This was the future!

ROSEMARY LANE

This is my home, this damp earth ditch, this ancient road. I cannot leave. I rest amongst the brambles and the woodland ferns, watching the changing seasons as the leaves of the trees that loom above me bud and fall. The fields to either side change from winter frost to meadow grass and beyond the village is still the same. But I don't think anyone remembers that there was once a road here, now bounded at either end by asphalt and fast metal that I dare not cross. I have become trapped, forgotten, alone with thoughts and memories that I wish were not mine.

I came upon the girl as she crouched on the damp earth and tangled tree roots of the bank, knotted hair and mud-scraped knees, hiding from her fellows whose laughter echoed across the field. She turned and saw me, and her face turned white like the mushrooms that burst from the leaf mould as the days shorten and the mist draws in. I could see the fear in her eyes, and I drew back into the thickets of thorns and nettles, watching her. She was the first person I had seen in the lane for many years, one of the village children, one of the innocents. I did not wish to frighten her, and I felt my loneliness rush in on me like a tide. But she fled, a scrabble of scuffed shoes on the loose stones and she was gone, running through the meadow grass and buttercups, scattering the sheep in her haste. I drifted back into the shadows and wallowed in remorse.

The girl must have told them about me, for the children came back, the boys leading the way, goading, teasing, daring each other to be brave, the girls hanging back in the long grass. They came up to the bank, laughing, throwing stones into the shadows, but stones can't hurt me, not any more. Then one of the boys dropped down into this ancient and forgotten road and beat the nettles with a stick, challenging me to show myself, and I could tell that his heart was bad.

And then they were gone, heading back across the meadow, their voices chanting in the breeze:

"Sally's a liar!"

"Sally thinks she saw a ghost!"

"Sally's scared of shadows!"

Sally.

The summers came and went and I watched her grow. Sometimes she glanced towards the thickets and shadows that shrouded Rosemary Lane, as if she knew I was watching her, and each time that happened something would flutter inside me, and I remembered how I had once known another girl, how I had once been happy.

Then one day something changed. There was a buzz in the air and blue lights flashing in the village through the dark and mist.

And with the dawn he came.

He was crouching amidst the ferns and tree roots, looking back across the fields towards the village, where she had been hiding all those years ago. And I sensed the blackness in his heart and the blood on his hands. And the blood was hers.

I felt a grief that I had never known in life, choking me with ice, blurring my vision with pain. Then the grief gave way to rage, slowly engulfing me as the flames of autumn fires consume dead leaves and wood. And I hated him. I remembered how he had shouted his challenge to the ferns and trees, his voice muffled by the damp earth. And I remembered another pain.

I had hung for my crimes from the gibbet at Bittery Cross. I remembered the death of another young maiden, and I wept for her for the first time in over a hundred years as I drifted amongst the ferns and fallen leaves towards him.

He turned and saw me then, but his eyes held no fear, and I saw that he was a kindred spirit. He was like me. Through the mist across the field, figures were moving in the grey dawn shrouds, at first indistinct and then drawing nearer. He knew they would not find him here. But I had found him first.

I reached towards him and heard the brittle crackle of his laugh, and he sensed my anger as I raged around him. If I had had a material body I would have killed him, but it was not for me to do. I saw the unease enter his eyes, just before he broke cover, running through the wet grass along the hedge, and I rested, and watched, aching inside. I watched him fall, I watched him die, as the sound of the gunshot echoed through the fields.

The years roll on and still I linger, watching the world from the shadow of the trees and ferns. Yet I am no longer alone here, in this abandoned lane of mud and leaves where no-one comes. He does not approach me, nor I him. But we both remember.

THE END

Fortean Fiction

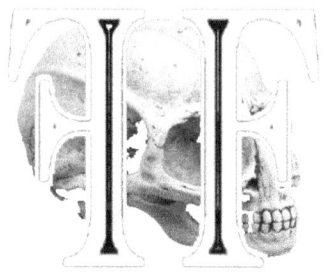

CFZ PUBLISHING GROUP

www.cfzpublishing.co.uk